# A LONG JOURNEY TO A NEW HOME

By

Esther Allen Peterson

Royal Fireworks Press

Unionville, New York

# For Kirsten, Keith, Kate, Luke, and especially Andrew

Library of Congress Cataloging-in-Publication Data

Peterson, Esther Allen.
  A long journey to a new home / by Esther Allen Peterson.
    p. cm.
  Summary: In the late nineteenth century, eleven-year-old Trygve Ytterhorn and his family leave their home in Norway and cross the Atlantic Ocean, hoping to find a better life in the Dakota Territory of America.
  ISBN-13: 978-0-88092-469-6 (library binding : alk. paper)
  ISBN-10: 0-88092-469-1 (alk. paper)
  ISBN-13: 978-0-88092-470-2 (pbk. : alk. paper)
  ISBN-10: 0-88092-470-5 (alk. paper)
  1. Norwegian Americans--Juvenile fiction. [1. Norwegian Americans--Fiction. 2. Immigrants--Fiction.] I. Title.
  PZ7.P4434Lon 2006
  [Fic]--dc22

                                        2006003264

Royal Fireworks Press
First Avenue, PO Box 399
Unionville, NY 10988-0399
(845) 726-4444
FAX: (845) 726-3824
email: mail@rfwp.com
website: rfwp.com
ISBN: 978-0-88092-469-6 [0-88092-469-1]  Library Binding
ISBN: 978-0-88092-470-2 [0-88092-470-5]  Paperback

Printed and bound in the United States of America by American citizens using vegetable-based inks on acid-free, recycled paper and environmentally-friendly cover coatings by the Royal Fireworks Printing co. of Unionville, New York.

Trygve pulled his hat down and his muffler up in an attempt to keep the cold out. He stopped and waited for his sister to catch up with him.

"If you don't hurry, we'll be frozen stiff before we get there," he said.

"I'm coming as fast as I can," said Signe. "It's hard walking when it's so dark."

"I'm sick of winter and darkness," said Trygve.

"It isn't fair," said Signe. "Oscar and Mari's cousin from Bergen told me they have daylight every day all winter, and up here we have more than three months of steady darkness."

"Lots of things aren't fair," said Trygve. "It's not fair that Oscar's family owns the land we live on, and Pa has to give him half of everything he grows and they're rich and fat and we don't have enough food to make it through the winter."

"Ma says we're almost out of wheat," said Signe.

"Yuk," said Trygve. "We're already out of potatoes. Soon it will be oatmeal and milk, and milk and oatmeal, and oatmeal and milk."

"And smoked fish," said Signe.

"Mustn't forget the fish," said Trygve.

They made their way around the last curve in the road that led to the schoolhouse. The schoolhouse was

1

silhouetted against a dark gray sky with pink and green lines descending and ascending upwards.

"The northern lights are bright," said Signe.

"It's like the world is attached to ropes and is swinging from heaven. That is, if there is a heaven," said Trygve.

Signe gasped. "What do you mean?" she said. "Of course there's a heaven."

"What makes you so sure?" asked Trygve.

"How dare you?" said Signe. "God might strike you dead for talking like that."

"Talking like how?" asked Oscar Dahl as he came around the corner of the schoolhouse.

"I said 'if there is a heaven,'" said Trygve. pulling his hat off and raising it toward the sky. "Have you ever thought about it? That there very well might not be a heaven or a hell or a God?"

"God might not strike you dead for saying that, but I'm sure Master Jensen will give it a try," said Oscar.

Just then Eric, Jon, and Egil joined them. "What will Master Jensen give a try?" asked Egil.

"He'll give Trygve the switch when he hears that he's been saying there's no God or heaven or hell," said Oscar.

"Who's going to tell him?" asked Trygve.

"You never know," said Oscar. "I might just have a chat with him before the day is out."

Lars Jensen, the schoolmaster, stood in the doorway of the schoolhouse with the bell in his hand. The light from the lanterns inside pushed back the darkness outside. Oscar stopped and talked to the schoolmaster as he passed through the doorway. Then he looked sideways at Trygve, who was now in the circle of light in front of the school.

Trygve put his coat and his lunch box, which contained two smoked fish, in the cloakroom. Then he went to his desk and slid under it as far as he could.

Master Lars Jensen stood in front of the class with a large Bible in his hands. "For this morning's scripture we will read from the fifty-third Psalm."

All of the students stood up for the reading of the scripture. Trygve looked at the window and wished it was springtime so he could see outside. He imagined the pink flowers blooming on the side of the mountain and the cascading waterfalls fed by the melting snow.

The schoolmaster began reading the Psalm, "The fool says in his heart, 'There is no God.' They are corrupt, doing abominable iniquity...."

Trygve looked at his feet. He felt his neck and ears turn warm.

When Master Jensen was through reading the Psalm, he closed the Bible and looked at Trygve. "I understand we have a student who says there is no God."

Trygve looked up. "I didn't say there is no God. I said there might not be a God. How can anyone be sure?"

"We can be sure because the Holy Bible says so," said the schoolmaster.

"But what about things that aren't fair? If there is a God, why do so many people die because they don't get enough to eat and others have so much to eat that they get fat?" Trygve looked hard at the teacher.

"I don't know the answer to your question, but I do know that you are committing blasphemy and that will not go unpunished in my classroom. Go into the cloakroom and drop your pants."

Trygve went into the cloakroom while Master Jensen took the switch from above the door. "Put your hands up on the shelf," ordered the schoolmaster.

Trygve hung onto the top shelf while the switch lashed against the backs of his knees. He bit his lip and counted to himself, ..*eight, nine, ten, eleven...* Usually when Master Jensen used the switch he gave only ten lashes. *He must be very angry,* said Trygve to himself.

After twenty lashes, the schoolmaster was finished and went back into the classroom. Trygve felt the welts rising up on the backs of his legs. He pulled up his trousers and went to his desk.

All of the students except for Oscar were looking down at their desks or at the floor. Oscar was looking straight at Trygve with a smug grin pasted on his face.

Trygve sat at his desk. Soon the students were caught up in their work. Trygve wrote on his slate, "I'LL GET YOU. JUST WAIT." Then he poked Oscar.

Oscar looked at the slate, and then Trygve quickly erased it.

○  ○  ○

Trygve and Signe walked up the path that led to the crofter's cottage. Soon they were past the trees. The dim light from inside interrupted the darkness of the afternoon.

"You won't tell," said Trygve to Signe.

"No, of course not," she said.

As they entered the cottage, their mother was pouring the oatmeal porridge into the large wooden bowl. Trygve didn't like the oatmeal but was glad for it. The dried fish that he took in his lunch box never filled the empty hole in his stomach. Rolf, who was three years old, quickly got his spoon and climbed up on the bench and stood between Trygve and Signe, and the three of them shared the bowl of porridge.

"Where's Pa?" asked Trygve.

"He went into the village," said Ma. "He should be home soon."

Before they were through eating, the door opened. Trygve's Pa came in and took off his fur hat and mittens. Then he took off his scarf and coat and hung them on the hook.

Jon Nels Ytterhorn was as tall as the doorway when he stood up and as narrow as a broomstick, so it seemed to Trygve. In his hand was a letter. He silently handed it to his wife. Then his eyes rested on Trygve. "Let me see your legs," he said.

*He would have to find out,* Trygve said to himself. He pulled up his pant legs to just above his knees.

5

"What did you do to deserve that?" asked Pa.

"I said that there might not be a God, and Oscar told on me."

"You have disgraced the good name of Ytterhorn," said Pa as he took off his belt.

"I didn't mean to," said Trygve. "I only said it to Signe and big ears Oscar snuck around the corner and heard me."

"That's true," said Signe.

"I don't think Trygve should be punished twice for the same sin," said Ma.

"He was punished for blasphemy," said Pa. "I aim to punish him for disgracing our family name." He looked at his son's legs for a minute. The red and blue welts were laced up and down his calves to his thighs. "You deserve another whipping but I think you've had enough for one day." He put his belt back on.

"Read the letter out loud," he said to Ma as he sat down at the table.

Trygve and Signe sat down on the bench by the door. It was only the second letter that had ever come to their family. Rolf, sensing the importance of the occasion, quit playing and climbed onto his Pa's lap.

Ma took the letter out of its envelope and walked over to the candle by the cupboard. She held the letter up to the candle. The light from the candle outlined her hair and danced in the shadows  She began to read:

To my dear cousin Jon and his wife Gro;

I am writing to try to persuade you and the children to come and join us in America. There are many Norwegians here. Most of them were very poor back in Norway as we were. Some of them didn't have enough money for their passage and had to borrow. But all of them and us have become well-to-do people. We all have land that belongs to us and have built ourselves good houses.

Everyone here also has a good amount of cows, and pigs, and chickens. I myself have four cows, twenty chickens, and eight pigs. This past year's crop was so plentiful that I had a surplus to sell. I got four hundred dollars for it and am sending you fifty to help pay for your passage should you decide to come to America. At first you could stay with us and get work. Then in a short time you could afford to buy your own land or go homesteading in the Dakota Territory. That's where the government is giving away land. You get one hundred and sixty acres free if you will live on it and raise crops. There are many Norwegians beginning to settle there now.

Gunhild and the children send you their love. We are all hoping you will come and join us here in America.

Your Cousin Elmer

"Let's go," said Trygve.

Pa, Ma, and Signe didn't say anything. They just sat there thinking. Finally Pa said, "Our situation is so hard here. I wonder if it is as good as Elmer says it is."

"One hundred and sixty acres," said Trygve. "I bet that's twice as much land as the Dahls have."

"But if we go across the ocean, we'll never see Grandma, or our aunts and uncles and cousins again," said Signe.

"If we don't go, we'll have to hire out Trygve when he turns twelve next summer," said Ma. "He'll have to go to work for the Dahls or the Sabes to help keep us from starving."

Trygve knew it was the custom for poor families to hire their children out, but he didn't say anything. He thought he would rather die than work for Oscar's father.

"I think we should go," said Ma. "There is no future here for us or our children. We can hardly raise enough to pay the rent and keep us alive through the winter and with another mouth to feed come summer..."

"You are right," said Pa. "But we have two months to think about it. We can't travel or have an auction till spring. Now let's go feed the goats."

When Pa and Trygve had finished milking, Trygve took a small pail of the warm milk and started for the big house. He detested taking the pail of milk every evening, but it was part of the rent they owed the Dahls, and it was Trygve's job to deliver it.

Even in the dark, he could see the house as he approached. It was large and painted shiny white with red shutters. It stood in sharp contrast to the weathered gray crofter's hut that they lived in. Every time Trygve saw it, he felt the unfairness of the world that he saw around him. Many lanterns were lit in the house, and light streamed through the windows upstairs and down, lighting up the pathway as Trygve approached the house.

Trygve knocked on the door and Oscar's mother opened it.

"Good evening," said Trygve. Mrs. Dahl took the pail from Trygve and closed the door without saying anything. As Trygve turned to leave Oscar jumped out from the barn.

"And how is the little milk boy?" said Oscar with a sneer.

"Looking for a bone to pick?" said Trygve. He knew he wanted to wallop him but certainly not in his own yard. It would be better done on the way to school. He looked away, and Oscar started for the house.

Trygve did not see Oscar put his foot in front of him. As Trygve fell to the ground, Oscar taunted him, "Why don't you watch where you're going?"

All of the anger and humiliation of the morning returned to Trygve, and he lunged at Oscar's leg and caught him before he could get to the house.

Oscar fell to the ground, and Trygve jumped on top of him. He took Oscar by the hair and smashed his face into the frozen ground. "Take that! And that! And that!!" he shouted.

At once Oscar's father was there. He pulled Trygve from on top of Oscar and Oscar got up. He had a cut on his forehead and his nose was bleeding.

"Ruffian!" cried Alfred Dahl. "You'll pay for this. This spring we'll find a new family to rent to, a family that's deserving."

"Go right ahead," retorted Trygve. "We're leaving anyway."

"Oh yeah?" said Oscar in disbelief. "Where are you going?"

"To America," said Trygve.

"What?" said Alfred Dahl.

"It's like I said," said Trygve. "We're going to America."

"You can't go," said Mister Dahl. "Your father is a good renter, and anyway he signed a renter's contract."

"Tough," said Trygve. He turned and headed for home. He hadn't ever felt so good. He hoped he wouldn't be in trouble for saying they were going to America. What if they didn't go?

But it surely felt good saying "tough" to Mister Dahl instead of tilting his hat and saying, "Good evening, Sir."

Every Sunday morning the Ytterhorn family attended church, and this Sunday morning was no exception, although Trygve wished it were. Trygve enjoyed the singing, but how he hated sitting through the sermon. Pastor Johanson always said that any pastor who was worth his salt could preach a two-hour sermon, and everyone knew that Pastor Johanson was worth his salt.

Today Trygve especially hated going to church because they would see Mr. Dahl, who would surely ask Pa if they were moving to America. And no one was supposed to know.

Jon Ytterhorn carried Rolf down the dark mountain path. Ma and Signe followed him, and Trygve lagged behind, kicking rocks down the mountain side. He caught up as they approached the church. The Hans Vogel family was entering the church at the same time.

Mr. Vogel said to Pa, "I hear you'll be heading for America."

"We're thinking about it," said Pa. He looked at Ma and then at Signe. Then they all looked at Trygve.

"I only told Oscar, and he promised not to tell," said Trygve.

Trygve slid into the pew, and Signe moved in next to him. In the winter they always sat close together to keep warm. Claus and Hilda Erickson and their eight children filled the pew in front of them.

11

Hilda turned around and spoke to Ma. "Are you really moving to America?"

"We are thinking about it," said Ma.

Trygve looked at the floor. "That's okay," said Ma. "The news would have gotten out sooner or later."

After the singing of the liturgy and hymns, Pastor Johanson climbed the steps up to the pulpit and from high above the congregation began to speak. "Before I begin my sermon I would like to comment on some distressing news that I heard this past week. I have heard that another family from our village is planning to leave Norway to go to America."

Trygve could feel everyone's eyes on them, and he slid further down in the pew. Pa, Ma, and Signe looked at the floor.

Pastor Johanson looked at the Ytterhorn family and then at the entire congregation. "I want to urge them and anyone else who is considering leaving our motherland to reconsider. Only those who are completely bereft of their senses would consider going to America where godlessness, sickness, and misery prevail. I have heard that immigrants are cheated every time they turn around and those who have left here have experienced difficulties that you could never dream of...."

Trygve squirmed and looked at his mother. Her face was red, and she continued looking at the floor. His father stared at the back of the next pew as the pastor went on and on. He wondered why the church and the landowners were so opposed to families leaving. Did they want the poor to stay poor forever?

After church a crowd gathered around them. It seemed to Trygve that almost everyone wanted to talk to them. The blacksmith took Pa's hand. "Jon," he said. "Norway is a poor and wretched land. I am glad you are going to America. I hope you will be happy and prosperous."

Nels Nelsen, another crofter, said, "Here we have to slave and suffer want. They say that everyone in America gets rich. I intend to go, too, as soon as my Martha is well."

Trygve looked up. His grandma and his Aunt Helen stood looking at his parents.

"We planned to tell you first," said Ma. "But Trygve told Oscar Dahl, and in two days the whole village and countryside knows."

"Are you really going?" asked Grandma.

"I think so," said Ma.

"We'll be over this afternoon," said Grandma.

As they were leaving the church, they stopped to talk to Rebekka, Ma's girlhood friend. Trygve had heard that before Pa had married Ma, he had been good friends with Rebekka. He had also heard that it was because Rebekka was so fond of Pa that she had never married. Nevertheless, Ma and Rebekka always delighted in seeing each other.

Now they spoke softly and tears ran down Rebekka's face. "Gro," she said. "All my life you have been my dearest friend. I will miss you."

"And I you," said Ma. "Perhaps you will come to America, too, someday."

"I doubt it," said Rebekka. "A new country is not a place for old maids." They both laughed.

"Well," said Ma. "We won't be leaving till spring. And that is a good six weeks away. We will see a lot of each other till then."

When they reached the bottom of the steps, they saw Mr. Dahl waiting to talk to Pa. "So you're planning on leaving us," he said.

"It's beginning to look that way," answered Pa.

"Maybe you should do some serious thinking about it," said Mr. Dahl. "You know you signed a renter's contract."

"That contract stipulates the conditions upon which we live on your land. It doesn't mention my leaving or how long I will work your land."

"We'll see," said Mr. Dahl as he climbed into his carriage.

"He doesn't scare me," said Pa. "I may be poor, but I'm not a fool."

Oscar came running to the coach as his father pulled on the reins of the horses. His face was bruised, and he had a sore on his forehead.

"Looks like Oscar had an accident," said Ma.

Trygve smiled at Signe, who was walking ahead with him.

"A person has to admit he had it coming," said Signe.

As they rounded a bend in the mountain path, they both saw it at the same time: the sun was back in the sky. The red ball of fire pushed its way over the top of the next mountain.

Trygve jumped and clicked his heels together. Ma and Pa and Rolf paused to watch the sun. It didn't stay long, but it brought a promise. The long dark night of winter was over.

The family was scarcely through with their supper when Grandma and Aunt Helen came up the pathway. Aunt Helen was the wife of Ma's oldest brother Nels, who was the heir to Trygve's grandparents' farm. It was the custom that the eldest son inherited the land, but there really wasn't enough land to divide anyway.

Trygve thought Aunt Helen acted like she thought she was better than his Ma and Pa because they were land owners—poor landowners, but landowners nevertheless.

Usually when Grandma came to their house, she took time to play with Rolf or talk to Trygve and Signe, but today she seemed to have a singleness of purpose. Trygve thought he knew what that purpose was. He figured she was going to try to persuade his parents to stay in Norway.

He climbed up into the loft so he could listen without being seen. He knew if he stayed downstairs he might get in trouble for speaking when he was supposed to be silent.

From the loft he watched his mother place the blue and white dishes and cups that had been wedding gifts on the table. Then she put cheese and dried fish on a plate. She worked in silence, and nobody said a word.

15

Finally Grandma stood up and said, "You know why I'm here."

"I have an idea," said Pa.

"You can't go," she said. "Gro will have her baby at sea."

Ma answered, "It shouldn't be any worse than having it here in this cottage."

"I have heard that immigrants have suffered untold hardships in America," said Aunt Helen. Trygve thought she sounded like Pastor Johanson.

"Read this letter from my cousin," said Pa.

Grandma took the letter from Uncle Elmer, and she and Aunt Helen sat on the bench by the table. Grandma placed the letter by the flickering candle and they began to read.

When they were through reading Grandma got up and paced back and forth. Then she stood still and said, "I can see why you want to go, but I don't think they have it that good."

"I don't think Elmer would lie to us," said Ma. She looked down at the floor and said, "Mama, you don't really know how bad it is for us. We never have enough food to make it through the winter. The reason there is no flat bread on the table is because we have just run out of wheat so there is no flour. A month ago we ran out of potatoes."

"Oh," said Grandma.

"And the future won't be any better," said Pa. "Our children will be poorer than we are. In America we will

16

have a large farm that will belong to us, and we will have a chance to become well-to-do people."

Then Ma looked her mother in the face and said, "If we stay another year, Trygve will have go to work for the Dahls or Sabes so that the food will go further."

"We didn't know you had it so bad," said Grandma. "We could help you out. We have a little wheat and potatoes to spare."

"But there's no hope for our children here," said Pa. "None at all."

Tears welled up in Grandma's eyes and spilled down her cheeks. Trygve wondered if Grandma's crying would make his parents change their minds. He remembered his Ma crying once and his Pa giving in to her.

Ma walked over to Grandma and held her in her arms, and they cried together. Finally Ma said, "It's something we have to do. It won't be easy for us to leave here and go to a new land, but we've got to give it a try."

Trygve looked at Signe, who was sitting by the fire. She was sniffling and wiping her eyes. Aunt Helen was staring at the fire and Pa was looking out the window.

Pa broke the silence. "I'm going out to check on the goats."

*The goats don't need any checking,* thought Trygve. *We don't milk for another two hours.*

Pa went out and closed the door.

"It's like we'll be losing all of you forever and ever," said Grandma.

"We will write letters to you," said Ma. "And perhaps we'll be so prosperous that we can come back for a visit sometime."

Grandma wiped her eyes and said, "This is enough carrying on. We'll just have to make the most of the next six weeks."

When Trygve and Signe arrived at school, their classmates gathered around them. Trygve felt important as everyone tried to talk to them at the same time.

"Are you really going to America?" asked Egil.

"Yah, you bet we're going," said Trygve. "And in a very short time we'll be very, very rich."

"What makes you so sure?" asked Oscar.

"Pa's cousin Elmer has been there for just three years and already has three times as much land as you do, and he has a hundred cows that all give a great amount of milk. They have twenty men who help with the milking, and they sell the milk and get hundreds of dollars for it every week."

Trygve looked at Signe. He knew she wouldn't let on that he was exaggerating.

The bell rang, and the children hurried to hang up their coats in the cloakroom. As Trygve slid into his desk, Master Jensen said, "So the Yrrerhorn family will be moving to America. I understand there is a great deal of godlessness and wickedness there. I do think Trygve should get along just fine in that country."

Trygve looked at his desk and pretended he didn't hear Master Jensen. When Master Jensen turned around to pick up the Bible, Trygve stuck his tongue out at him. Helen, who sat next to him, laughed.

Master Jensen turned around quickly and asked, "Is there something funny going on that I should know about?"

Trygve just stared at his desk, hoping that Helen wouldn't tell on him. He breathed a sigh of relief when she didn't say anything. If Oscar had seen him and told, he surely would have felt the switch again.

◯ ◯ ◯

When they arrived home that afternoon, a trunk sat in the middle of the cottage floor. The lid was open, and on the bottom of it were two intricately stitched tablecloths that Ma had made when she was a girl. On top of the tablecloths was a pair of candlestick holders that had been a gift to Ma and Pa when they were married.

"This is our America trunk," said Ma. "Most everything we are taking will go in here."

"Even our food?" asked Signe.

"No," said Ma. "Just our household things and clothing. Pa is making a cask for the food and a box for the spinning wheel and the tools."

"And a box for the baby," said Pa, who was busy sawing boards.

"Why a box?" asked Signe.

"Because the cradle won't work on the ship," said Pa. "I'll build another cradle after we get to America."

As each day passed, the sun stayed in the sky a little longer, and new items were packed in the America trunk. Trygve's excitement grew. He was ready for an adventure and couldn't wait for his family to be rich.

The sun was high in the sky as Trygve and his family made their way down the mountain path to the church. Pink and white flowers dotted the mountainside, and great waterfalls, fed by the melting snow, cascaded into the valley below.

"These six weeks have gone so fast," said Ma.

"Yes," said Pa.

"Are you nervous?" she asked.

"A little," he replied.

"All of a sudden I feel lonely and scared."

"You can still change your mind." said Pa.

"No," said Ma. "It's just that I feel sad going to this church for the last time. The children were all baptized here, and our Marta and little Anton are buried here."

"Yes," said Pa. "Our lives and our parents' lives and their parents' lives were centered on this church. More than two hundred years of our family's history is recorded in its books."

As they approached the church, Erik Hanson, a retired army colonel, stepped up to Pa. "You'll be leaving us soon?" he asked.

"We're planning to leave on Wednesday," answered Pa.

The Colonel looked into Pa's eyes and gripped his hand while he spoke to him. "God go with you," he said. "I hear the land is fertile there and wages are high. In America fortune smiles on the humble, and all are equal before the law."

Another crofter stopped to talk with Pa. "I wish I had the courage to go," he said. "You write and tell us if it's as good as they say it is. Then maybe I'll come next year."

They went into the church and filed into their family's pew. Sunshine streamed through the windows as they sat listening to the organ. Trygve looked sideways at his Ma and saw a tear slide down her cheek.

During the service the pastor announced, "This coming week the Jon Ytterhorn family will be leaving for America. Their auction will be held on Wednesday if it is not raining. In the event of rain, it will be held the first day thereafter that it is not raining. We wish them God's blessing in this undertaking. We hope that they will not be lured away from the faith of their forefathers in America, where I have heard that extreme wickedness and godlessness prevail."

After church they walked to the graveyard and stood by the two small graves marked by one headstone. They stood there and didn't say anything. They just remembered. If Trygve's sister, Marta, had lived, she'd be eight now, and Anton would have been five. They both died the same week when Anton was a baby.

○  ○  ○

On Tuesday, Trygve didn't go to school. He gathered the goats and took them to feed higher up the mountain. As he climbed, he looked off into the hazy distance at the school, at the village below, at the grand houses, and the crofters' huts. He looked at the villages nestled on the sides of the mountains and at the deep blue fjords that outlined the valleys and divided the mountains. He wondered if there would be fjords like these in the Dakota Territory.

Trygve looked at the goats. For the first time in his life, he felt a genuine fondness for them. "Dumb animals," he said. "If it weren't for your milk, we might have starved last winter." He bent over and patted the lead goat on the head and said, "Daisy, you're a good girl."

When they reached a small meadow, he sat down on the ground and picked a small white flower. He looked at it as though it were the only flower that had ever grown.

When the sun began to slide down the mountain, Trygve started to lead the goats down the rocky slope. As he approached the hut, he could see that everything was ready for the auction. The plowshare was cleaned and lined up with the wagon and tools.

Inside the house, the furniture was polished. The little farm and its people were waiting for tomorrow.

Trygve had a hard time falling asleep that night, and almost immediately he heard his Pa saying, "Today is the day. Open up your eyes and hop to it."

As soon as Trygve's feet hit the floor, Pa pulled the covers from the bed and threw them down to Ma, who folded them and put them in the America trunk.

"Help me with the beds," said Pa as he went down the ladder. Trygve pushed his bed over the side of the loft, and Pa lowered it and carried it outside. Soon the four beds were lined up next to the plow, and Trygve went inside to eat his oatmeal.

Next Trygve carried out the cradle that all five children had slept in when they were babies. Then he helped Pa carry out the stove, cupboard, table, and benches. With reluctance he carried out the rocking chair. It was a beautiful chair with carved birds in flight on its back. Trygve's great grandma had given it to Ma and Pa for a wedding gift. Ma had always sat in it when she nursed her babies, and he and Signe called it "Ma's rocker."

Soon the auctioneer, a man called Lucas, came and looked over everything. "Not an awful lot here," he said. "But we'll try to get a good price for it."

"I hope so," said Pa. "We need enough to get us to America."

The neighbors and people from town began to arrive. They milled around, looking at the pots and pans and trying out the beds. One fat lady from town sat down in the rocker, and Trygve was afraid it might break. Two men felt the udders and ribs of each of the goats.

The auctioneer climbed up on the wagon, and everybody stopped talking. He held up one of the blue and white dishes. "What am I offered for these fine dishes?" he asked.

"One krone," said a voice in the crowd.

"Only one krone?" asked the auctioneer. "These are worth at least twenty kroner."

Finally someone said, "Two kroner."

The auctioneer said, "Sold for two kroner."

"We'll never have enough money to get to America," said Trygve.

"We'll manage, somehow," said Pa. He looked disappointed.

"That's okay," said Ma. "They're only dishes."

"Your good dishes," Signe reminded her.

Then the auctioneer held up the small sugar bowl and creamer and four cups and saucers. They were white with blue birds and pine trees and had been a wedding gift. Ma had not wanted to put them on the auction but was afraid they would just end up broken.

Rebekka was standing in the back of the crowd and put her finger up. "One kroner," she said.

"Sold," said the auctioneer.

Rebekka took the box with the delicate pieces of china in it and walked over to where Gro, Signe, and Trygve were standing.

"I will always treasure these," she said. "It will be a constant reminder of you."

"I'm glad you got them," said Ma smiling.

Rebekka and Ma stood together talking. They laughed and they cried. Rebekka turned to Trygve and Signe and said, "I hope you'll be very happy in America." Then she wiped away a tear and left.

It was so strange for them watching everything from their home being carried away. And things were going so cheap.

The last thing to be sold was the rocking chair. The auctioneer held it up and put it down again. "What am I offered for this fine carved rocker?"

The fat lady said, "One krone."

"Two kroner," said Nels Haug.

Two more men bid a few times and then dropped out. It went back and forth between the fat lady and Nels Haug. "Eight kroner," she said.

"Nine kroner," said Nels Haug.

"Ten."

It was Nels Haug's turn to bid. He turned and talked to his wife and then bid again. "Eleven kroner," he said.

"Twelve." said the fat lady.

Nels Haug conferred with his wife again, and then he shook his head.

"Sold to Mrs. Thorvold Jensen for twelve kroner," said the auctioneer.

Trygve wished that the Haugs could have gotten the rocking chair. "Mrs. Jensen probably has six rocking chairs already," he said to Signe.

"At least we got a good price for it," said Signe. A tear ran down Ma's face as the rocker was carried to the Jensen wagon.

Later, as the goats were led away, Trygve felt like part of himself was going with them. As each one of their belongings was taken away, it seemed to Trygve that a piece of life as he had known it went with it. But he reminded himself that it was all for a good reason. Soon they would be very, very rich.

Almost too soon, the auction was over, and the neighbors and relatives crowded around them to wish them well. Ma hugged her cousins, sisters, and Grandma.

Trygve's uncles, Lars and Oscar, helped Pa load the America trunk, the box with the spinning wheel and a few tools in it, and the two casks of food onto the wagon. Whenever Trygve saw his Pa and his uncles together, he wondered how three men could look so much alike and not be triplets. All three of them had straight blond hair, long thin noses, wide mouths, and large hands with long skinny fingers.

Signe and Rolf climbed up onto the wagon with the men, and Trygve went back into the house to see what was keeping his Ma. He stepped softly. He didn't want to interrupt his Ma's remembering.

He went to her and stood quietly by her side, and then looked up into her face. Tears rolled down her cheeks. He had to swallow hard to hold back his own tears.

Ma put her arm around Trygve's shoulder and pointed to where the bed had stood and said, "That's where you and Signe and Rolf and the others were born." Then she pointed to the corner behind where the rocker had stood. "That's where you liked to play when you were a tiny little boy."

They stood for a moment, saying a silent farewell to the humble crofter's hut that had been their home. "We've lingered long enough," said Ma. "It's time to go." They went outside and closed the door of the weathered cabin for the last time.

Pa gave Ma his hand, and she climbed up onto the wagon. Trygve put his hand on the side of the wagon and jumped up. Pa and his uncles sat in the front. Ma, Signe, and Rolf sat on the boards that were strung across the back of the wagon, while Trygve sat on top of the box.

Ma put her arm around Signe, who was already feeling lonesome. "See here now," she said. "You'll make new friends fast, and there'll be Cousin Elmer and Gunhild and Sven and Mari."

Soon they came to the first crossroads. They looked to the right, toward the church, and kept going straight ahead. A crofter who was bent over in a field straightened up and waved his hand and shouted, "Good luck. May all your dreams come true."

Trygve looked at the crofter's field of sprouting oats and rocks and said, "In America the land will be rich, and there won't be any rocks to pick."

Slowly the wagon made its way down the mountainside to the fjord below. It stopped at a fishermen's wharf, and Trygve and his uncles started unloading their belongings onto the dock.

Pa walked up to a fisherman whose boat was loaded with fish. "Will you be heading toward Bergen shortly?" he asked.

The fisherman answered, "We'll be going that direction as soon as the fish are spread."

"Would you have room for us and our cargo?" asked Pa.

"I reckon we can make room," he answered, and Pa handed him a coin. "No," said the fisherman. "You'll need it when you get there."

"Thank you," said Pa, and he and Trygve and the uncles started loading their things onto the boat.

Rolf looked at the fishing boat and said, "I thought we were taking a big boat across the ocean."

"We are," said Pa. "But first we have to get to it."

When the small boats that were towed by the larger boat were full of fish, the fisherman heaved up the sails while the uncles gave the boat a shove. The Ytterhorn family waved goodbye to Lars and Oscar until they could hardly see them anymore. A gust of wind caught the sails, and they were pulled down the fjord toward the sea, and Oscar and Lars faded into the scenery on the banks of the fjord.

Ma leaned against the America trunk and fell asleep. Rolf took his blanket and curled up on the floor. The sun was warm, and Trygve felt himself drifting off. Soon he was on the floor next to Rolf. When he awoke, they had left the fjord, and strong ocean breezes were moving them swiftly down the coast.

At Bode the fishing boat pulled up to a wharf. "This is as far as we go," said the fisherman. "You'll have to take the steamer the rest of the way."

Trygve helped his father unload the America trunk, the casks, and the box onto the dock. He watched as the fishing boat pulled away, "I hope the steamer comes soon," he said.

For more than an hour his Pa and Ma paced back and forth, and Signe chased Rolf. "I hope we don't have to wait till tomorrow," said Ma.

The evening air became cool, and Rolf and Signe snuggled against Ma, trying to keep warm. Trygve stood on a pile of lumber and boxes and scanned the horizon. Then he turned around and looked up the fjord.

"I see it," he shouted, pointing excitedly.

Signe stood up and looked. "I don't see anything except a cloud of black smoke," she said.

"That's it," said Trygve. "Steamboats make smoke."

An hour later the steamboat pulled into port.

Pa paid the captain for passage to Bergen, and he and Trygve carried the trunk up the gangplank and placed it on the floor of the boat with other families and their trunks and casks.

"This part of the boat is called the steerage," said a well-dressed boy who was about Trygve's age. "It's where the poor people get to ride."

31

Trygve didn't pay any attention as he hurried back with his Pa to get the casks and the box. He didn't care that they were poor now. Soon they would be rich. Very, very rich.

Once on the boat, Ma took cheese, dried fish, and flatbread from the casks. The family sat in a small circle and ate their supper. Then Ma took two feather ticks from the trunk and spread them out for her family. Pa, Ma, Signe, and Rolf curled up on the feather ticks, but Trygve decided to look around. There was so much to see. There were men feeding a huge furnace that made boiling water that turned into steam and made the paddle wheel go around. He had never seen anything like it.

Then he stood at the railing and watched the lights coming on in the towns that they passed. The boy who spoke to him while they were boarding came and stood next to him. "How long till we get to Bergen?" he asked.

"Someone told me two or three days," said the boy. "It depends on how much stopping we do."

"Hmm," said Trygve. "Two or three days. I may as well get some sleep." He went and laid down between his Pa and the America trunk.

○　○　○

Three days later, on Saturday afternoon, Trygve saw Bergen. He had probably seen more than a hundred towns and villages along the coast, but he knew this had to be

Bergen. It was big, and in its harbor sat four large sailing ships.

When the steamer had finally docked, Trygve helped his Pa with the trunk, the box, and the casks. Then he sat on the dock with his Ma and Signe and Rolf while Pa went to inquire about passage.

There was so much to see. Even Rolf, who was perplexed by the strange events of the past week, stopped whining. There were sailors hauling cargo, and merchants scurrying about doing business, and the sailing ships bobbing in the harbor.

More than a hundred families like theirs, with their scant belongings in their America trunks and boxes, were huddled on the dock waiting to board the ships and leave poverty behind. Trygve wondered if everyone who went to America would get rich. He was sure of one thing. They would.

In about half an hour Pa came back and said, "We'll be sailing on the *Franklin*. We can board now, and it will be taking off in a few hours." Once again Trygve helped his Pa with their cargo.

As they stepped onto the ship, the first mate came up to Pa and said, "I'll show you your quarters." Pa and Trygve followed him down the ladder to the hold. "There you go, sir," he said.

When the mate left, Trygve said to his Pa, "This is really small. Will we all fit?"

"You and Signe and Rolf can have the top bunk, and Ma and I will take the bottom." Together they squeezed the box and the trunk between the bunk and the wall. Then they put the casks on top.

Signe and Rolf looked at their sleeping compartment. "It's dark," said Signe.

"And it smells," said Rolf.

"And we'll manage," said Ma as she took the feather ticks out of the trunk and spread them over the two cots. Then she lay down while the others went exploring.

They came to a kitchen area where two women were cooking supper for their families. Then they went up on the main deck, and Trygve watched two boys who weren't much older than himself climbing high up on a mast to let down a sail. An older sailor stood below, pulling some ropes and yelling instructions up to them.

When they got back to their quarters, Ma was sitting on the bed. "I reckon everyone is getting hungry. I'll find the cooking area and make us some oatmeal."

"We already found it," said Signe. Ma followed her to the two black cooking stoves just below the main deck. When the oatmeal was done, they returned to their quarters, and the five of them ate from the pan in which it was cooked.

When Trygve was finished eating, he went back up on deck. All of the sails were in place, and the sailors were tying the ropes. The sails made flapping noises in the breeze and little by little began to catch the wind and billow. Very slowly they began to move. The sailing ship with a hundred and forty hopeful emigrants began its sweep out to sea.

The emigrants lined up along the railing of the ship to say farewell to Norway. Rolf sat upon his Pa's shoulders. "Take a good look," said Pa. "It's the last we'll ever see of our homeland." A tear rolled down Ma's face, and then Signe began to cry.

"Don't cry, " said Trygve. "Soon we'll be rich."

"I don't know about rich," said Pa. "But we should do better than in Norway."

"At least we will have hope," said Ma. "That's been the hardest thing. Not having any hope."

Trygve watched the steeples and red roof tops that dotted the side of a mountain. Almost all of the emigrants kept watch until their homeland faded into the hazy distance. Then one by one they filed down into the hold, but Trygve stayed longer. He was too excited to try to sleep. Finally, he went down into the hold, quietly slipped into his family's compartment, and climbed up onto the top bunk.

He laid awake for a long time listening to the night sounds. He could hear his mother breathing, and the waves breaking against the ship. Then there was someone snoring in the quarters just above them, and a woman across from them kept groaning and mumbling in her sleep. After what seemed like hours, Trygve fell asleep.

When Trygve awakened, he heard footsteps on the deck above him. Quietly he slid off the bunk, down to the edge of the trunk, then down to the floor. He stepped out of his family's quarters, climbed up to the deck, and went to the railing. There was no land to be seen anywhere. They were on the high seas.

After he had stood there for about five minutes, a man wearing a black uniform and a captain's hat came over to him. "Good morning" he said. "I'm Captain Vigen."

"I'm Trygve Ytterhorn."

"We're happy to have you on board. Do you have any questions?"

"Yes," said Trygve. "How long will it take us to get to America?"

"We are not going to America," said the captain. "We will be landing in Quebec, Canada. Then those going on to the United States can take another ship or a train to get to their destinations."

"Well, then how long will it take to get to Canada?"

"That's anybody's guess," answered the captain. "Our best time ever was five weeks and two days. Then once we had a terrible crossing. Took thirteen weeks. We had a whole week without a breath of wind and didn't move a knot. Then we had two storms that blew us way off course."

"Do you think this will be a good, fast trip?" asked Trygve.

"We're surely hoping so," said the captain. Then he looked at Trygve and asked, "How old are you?"

"I'll be twelve in a couple of weeks," answered Trygve.

"Almost old enough to rig a sail," said the captain, and he turned and walked to the stern of the ship.

Soon four boys and three girls came up on the deck. A tall boy with red hair came over to Trygve and said, "My name's Ole. Do you want to play Barber of Seville with us?"

"Sure," said Trygve.

"I'll be the barber. You hide."

Soon Signe came to get Trygve for breakfast.

As they ate the oatmeal Pa asked, "What have you been doing, Trygve?"

"Playing Barber of Seville," said Trygve. "It's great fun on a ship."

"I bet there's no end of places to hide," said Ma.

"I hear music," said Signe.

As soon as they were through eating, they went up on deck where a man was playing a salmodeker and a lady was pumping her accordion. "This looks like fun, " said Signe as she sat down on the deck floor.

Trygve looked at his parents. Ma was sitting on a box with Pa standing next to her. They were laughing and clapping their hands to the music. He couldn't remember them ever having so much fun.

The singing became more and more boisterous:

> *"I'm off to Oleana, I'm turning from my doorway,*
> *No chains for me, I'll say goodbye to slavery*
> *in old Norway.*
> *Ole-Ole-Ole- oh! Oleana!*
> *Ole-Ole-Ole- oh! Oleana!*

Trygve looked at his parents again. They looked younger, and were singing loudly. For the first time that Trygve could remember, the worried looks were gone from their faces.

> *"They give you land for nothing in jolly Oleana,*
> *And grain comes leaping from the ground in floods*
> *of golden manna.*
> *Ole- Ole- Ole- oh! Oleana!*
> *Ole- Ole- Ole- oh! Oleana!"*

On the twenty-second day at sea, Trygve was standing next to the captain and some of the sailors when he saw it. One long dark grey cloud was on the western horizon, and it was rolling toward them.

"It looks like a bad one," said the captain.

"It's coming fast," said an older sailor.

The captain yelled out with a sense of urgency, "Reef the sails. Hurry!"

Trygve watched the young sailors scamper up the masts. They went so fast he wondered if their lives depended upon it. Once they reached the tops, they took hold of the sails, lifted them away from the masts and started rolling them with steady coordination..

When the sails were halfway up, the captain raised his arms, the boys stopped their rolling and the older sailors tied them off. "Stay," yelled the captain. "We got to see what this storm's going to do."

The children stopped playing games, and the adults ceased their visiting and their singing. They all stood watching the menacing cloud and the frantic sailors.

The captain yelled, "Everyone down in the hold." Mothers and fathers started herding their children down the steep steps. But Trygve stayed on the deck, clutching the railing and watching.

The waves turned into mountains, and Trygve was sure they would be swallowed up by the sea, but the *Franklin* climbed up one side of the wall of water and came swooping down the other.

He was afraid for the young sailors who were clinging to the masts. "This is a bad one," said the captain to the crew. "Roll them all the way and make them tight," he yelled, and the boys on the masts once again began rolling the sails faster and faster.

The captain looked at Trygve and ordered, "Get to your quarters, boy."

Trygve made his way to the stairs, but couldn't help but watch the unfolding drama. He stood on the fourth step while the *Franklin* tilted from side to side. He watched the sailors tie off the sails and slide down the mast, to the deck. Then they raced towards the hold.

There was terror in the captain's eyes as he said, "Batten down the hatches. We're going to have to ride this one out."

Trygve quickly jumped down ahead of them and made his way down to his family's quarters. As he entered their compartment, the ship lurched sideways, Trygve fell down, and the casks fell on his head. Feeling blood gushing from his forehead, he took a cloth from the box and pressed it against his head.

Ma said, "Trygve, are you alright?"

"Ya," said Trygve as he passed out.

When he came to, he didn't know how long he had laid there, but his head had stopped bleeding. He climbed up into his bunk next to Rolf.

First the ship rolled in one direction, and Trygve and Rolf were thrown on top of Signe, who was by the wall. Then it rolled the other way, and Rolf and Signe were thrown up against Trygve. If not for the board on the side of the bunk, they would have all landed on the floor.

"I'm scared," said Rolf.

"It's just a storm," said Trygve. "We'll be alright." It was reassuring to Rolf, but Trygve wished he could believe it. All he could think about was the terror in the captain's eyes.

The stench of vomit filled the hold. It ran down the wall from above them, and Trygve listened to the heaving on both sides of them and from his parents below him. He buried his face in the feather tick, trying to calm his own stomach by smelling the blanket instead of the putrid air.

The ship cracked and creaked so loudly that Trygve was sure it was breaking apart and they would all be drowned. From somewhere in the hold a soft voice cried out, "Father in heaven, have mercy on our souls." Another person repeated it. The prayer spread quietly throughout the emigrants' quarters. Trygve listened as his parents joined in, "Father in heaven, have mercy on our souls."

Trygve found himself praying, "God up in heaven, if you are real we sure do need for you to save us," and with his face pressed into the feather tick he fell asleep.

When he awoke it was still, and sunlight poured into the hold. "It's awfully still," said Trygve.

"Too still," said Pa. "It doesn't feel like we're moving."

Trygve jumped down and hastened up to the deck. Ole was already on deck. The main mast with its sail still tied to it laid on the deck in pieces.

"It's all busted up," said Ole.

Together they watched the ship's carpenters carry lumber to rebuild the mast.

"It doesn't matter that the sails aren't up," said Trygve.

"Why?" asked Ole.

"There's no wind," said Trygve. "It's like glass out there."

"Look," said Ole. "They're taking a boat out. I wonder what for?"

"They've got spears," said Trygve. "I bet they're going to catch that little whale." He pointed at a twelve-foot blue whale it as it came up from the murky deep and dove down again.

The passengers gathered at the railing and watched. After two hours they had it. They threw more harpoons into it and together the sailors and the emigrants pulled it up onto the deck.

When evening came the main mast was up again, the sails were in place, and a gentle breeze filled them. They were on their way.

Trygve sniffed and said, "I can't wait till that whale is ready."

"They say there's plenty for everybody," said Ole.

A line of hungry people formed, each one holding a plate and a fork. Soon Trygve and his family sat on the deck enjoying the feast.

"This is the best meat I've had in years," said Ma.

"It's the only meat we've had in years," said Pa laughing.

Ma groaned and Trygve looked at her. She winced and held her abdomen.

Pa looked at her quickly. His concern showed in his face.

"It's time," said Ma.

After the feast of whale was over, the lady with the accordion began playing. Soon she was joined by the salmodeker player and two fiddlers.

Trygve watched his parents as they clapped and sang. Every now and then Ma clasped her abdomen and leaned forward. Finally she said, "I think I better go lay down."

"I'll get the midwife," said Pa. He went over to an older woman. When Pa spoke to her, she nodded her head and stopped singing. She got up from the deck where she was sitting and went with Pa.

That evening Trygve didn't play Barber of Seville. He stood at the railing looking out over the ocean and waited. He watched Signe trying to entertain Rolf. She was waiting, too.

An hour later Signe said, "Let's go down and see what's happening." When they got to their compartment the curtain that served as a door was closed. They stood outside and listened to their Ma moaning.

"I hope everything is okay," whispered Signe.

"Me, too," echoed Trygve and Rolf.

They went back up on deck and Trygve resumed his post, scanning the vast ocean while engrossed in his own deep thoughts. He watched two whales surface and dive and saw an iceberg in the distance.

Soon Signe ran over to him and said, "The midwife is back up here."

"It must be born now," said Trygve. "I wonder what it is?"

Trygve grabbed Rolf and the three of them tore across the full length of the deck and went down into the hold to their quarters. They tiptoed into the berth where Ma was lying with the baby next to her. They were both asleep, and Pa sat watching them.

"It's a girl," he said. "Her name is Carrie."

Trygve looked at baby Carrie. He didn't remember Rolf ever being that small. Her ears, nose, and fists were the tiniest he had ever seen. "I'm glad it's a girl," he said. "Our family is just right now. A mother and father and two boys and two girls, and when we get to America we will all get rich."

○ ○ ○

Two days later Signe carried baby Carrie up on deck. They were followed by Trygve and Ma. "The fresh air smells so good," said Ma. "It's so stale down in the hold."

Ma sat down on a crate and watched Rolf play games with the younger children. After a while she said, "Trygve!"

Trygve looked at her. She had become pale and shivered.

"I feel faint," she said. "I need to go and lie down."

Trygve helped her down into the hold. He thought she felt warm. By evening it was obvious that she had a fever.

At suppertime Signe and Trygve made the oatmeal and took it down to Ma. "Here," said Signe. "Eat some and get strong."

**44**

"No," said Ma. "I just want some water."

Trygve took the tin cup and filled it with water. She only took a few sips, and then she handed it to Pa. Pa just sat there holding her hand. He had a worried look on his face.

Very early in the morning Baby Carrie's crying awoke Trygve, Signe, and Pa. But Ma was not aware of her baby's crying. She called for her mother back in Norway.

Pa put his hand on Ma's forehead. He winced and whispered, "Oh, God!!" Then he went up onto the deck.

"He's gone to get the midwife," said Trygve. Then he climbed down by Ma and took her hand and held it. It was very warm and overly dry.

Signe held the crying baby and rocked back and forth, faster and faster. She bit her lip and fought back tears.

The midwife entered their compartment and stood over Ma. She felt her head and said, "Can you talk to me, Mrs. Ytterhorn?" But Ma didn't answer. She just looked at her with a wild, glassy stare.

The midwife stood up straight and looked at Pa with a pained expression. "I'm afraid she has the childbirth fever," she said softly.

"Oh, no, no, no!!" said Pa.

"You'll have to get a wet nurse for the baby," said the midwife. Then she looked at Signe, who was still rocking the squalling baby and said, "Take the baby to Mrs. Nielson. She has enough milk for two babies."

"Tell her that you will help her with her children if she will nurse Carrie," said Pa.

Signe put Carrie in the little wooden box and left to find Mrs. Nielson.

Trygve took Rolf and went up to make the morning oatmeal while Pa stayed with Ma. Never in his entire life had Trygve been so scared or felt so helpless

"Please, God!" he prayed. "Don't let her die."

○ ○ ○

For the next four days Ma laid in the Ytterhorn berth in the hold of the ship. She seemed to get hotter and hotter. At first she was delirious, and then she just slept a deep sleep. Trygve watched his father bend over her and wipe her brow and cheeks with a cool cloth. He wondered if Ma could feel Pa's tears falling on her face.

Early in the morning, when baby Carrie was six days old, Trygve awoke. He bent over and looked down into his parents' bunk. Pa was gone. He slid over the rail down to the cot below and sat by his Ma. With a feeling of dread, he reached out and touched her. She was cold.

He quickly got dressed and ran up on deck. Pa was speaking to the captain. Trygve walked up to them, and Pa reached over to him and pulled him close. Then Pa turned away from Trygve and went back down into the hold.

Trygve walked over to the side of the ship and stood looking out over the water. He sobbed and wiped at the tears that were spilling down his face. Then he felt an arm on his shoulder. It was the captain.

"You mustn't cry," said the captain. "It's the Lord's will when a person dies, and we musn't question the will of the Lord." Then he left, and Trygve was alone.

"If it's God's will that Ma died, then I hate God," he said under his breath. He looked up at the sky and shouted, "I HATE YOU, GOD." Then he looked around nervously, half expecting a bolt of lightning to come out of the blue and strike him dead. But nothing happened.

The captain and the ship's carpenter came by with a wooden box. Trygve knew what their business was and followed them down into the hold to get Ma.

Trygve watched as Pa gently lifted her body and laid it in the box. They stood there in silence, looking at her and remembering. Then Pa motioned to Trygve to pick up one end of the box and they carried her up and set her down on the deck.

The word of Ma's death had spread throughout the ship, and the emigrants gathered around her body for a funeral. The captain led them as they recited the Twenty-third Psalm. Then the musicians began to play "Who Knows When My Last Hour Cometh." Trygve remembered that song being sung at Martha and Anton's funeral. A few voices sang the hymn softly, but Trygve and his family just listened.

Next everyone joined together in saying the Lord's Prayer. Then four sailors came and poured pails of sand on Ma's body, covering her half way, and the ship's carpenter nailed down the lid. Then the four sailors picked up the crude coffin and lowered it overboard. It was all strangely quiet and solemn.

Ma's family stood by the railing and watched as the waves gently covered the coffin.

Trygve spent the next three weeks watching Rolf, making the oatmeal, and gazing at the vast, lonely ocean. Signe stayed busy taking care of baby Carrie and helping Mrs. Nielson with her four small children, and Pa sat on a cask in the stern of the ship, thinking. Except for Rolf, they neither played nor sang anymore.

"Trygve," said Signe, coming up behind him.

He turned around and looked at her holding the baby. "She's growing," he said.

"The midwife was right," said Signe. "Mrs. Nielson does have enough milk for two babies."

Rolf came over and asked, "Can I hold Carrie?"

"Only if you sit down," said Signe. Rolf sat down on the deck with his legs straight out, and Signe put Carrie in his arms. Soon he was tired of holding her and handed her back to Signe. Then he said, "Nothing's any fun anymore."

"No, it isn't," said Trygve.

"We haven't played any games or sung any songs since Ma died," said Signe.

"There's nothing to sing about," said Trygve.

"Ma wouldn't want it to be that way," she said.

"I guess you're right," said Trygve. "But I can't help it. It's like everything I have hoped for died with Ma. I don't even care if we never get rich."

"Ma didn't either," said Signe. "She just wanted for us to have enough so we wouldn't be hungry."

"And she wanted for us to have our own land so we wouldn't be beholden to people like Mr. Dahl," said Trygve. "I guess that's all we really need."

"You know," said Signe. "If we were to get rich, maybe we would act like the Dahls."

"We wouldn't want that to happen," said Trygve.

Pa walked up to his family. He reached out his hands and put one each on Trygve and Signe's shoulders. "I've been thinking," he said.

"About what?" asked Signe.

"About us," said Pa. "It's going to be awfully hard being a family without a mother."

"It already is," said Trygve.

"I'm going to write to Rebekka and ask her to come and keep our family together."

"What?" asked Signe.

"I think she will come," said Pa. "She loved your Ma more than anyone else. She'll do it for her."

"She can't take the place of our Ma," said Trygve.

"Nobody can ever take her place," said Pa. "But she is good and kind, and in time we will grow to love her."

"Not like Ma," said Trygve.

"No, not like your Ma," said Pa. "We will love her differently."

"How many kinds of love are there?" asked Signe.

"As many kinds as there are people," answered Pa.

Trygve and Signe didn't say anything at first. Then Signe said, "I guess it will be better than no mother."

"Now I am going to see if the captain has some paper I can use," said Pa turning to leave. "I need to write to your grandma, too."

Trygve walked back and forth in front of the captain's quarters. Pa was sitting at the captain's desk writing his letters. Trygve waited for a long time. When Pa came out he looked haggard, as though writing the letters had been a terrible strain.

He handed the letters to Trygve. He read the first one out loud:

*Dear Grandmother and Helen,*

*It is with great sadness that I write to you. On May twenty-second Gro had a baby girl. We named her Carrie and she is very pretty and healthy. When the baby was three days old, Gro came down with childbirth fever and died three days later. We buried her at sea.*

*I have blamed myself many times, but the midwife reminds me that it could have happened at home, too.*

*We hope you are well. I will write to you again after we arrive at Cousin Elmer's.*

Jon Ytterhorn

When Trygve finished reading the letter, he looked at Pa. His face was full of pain. Signe handed Carrie to Pa, and he looked down at her little face and smiled for the first time since Ma had died.

"She surely is beautiful," said Pa. "She's Ma's last gift to us."

Trygve handed the other letter to Signe. She opened it slowly and began to read it:

Dear Rebekka,

A terrible tragedy has overtaken us. After our baby Carrie was born, Gro got the childbirth fever and died.

I have always admired you because you are a good and honest woman. I know it is asking a lot but I am wondering if you would come to America and marry me and be a mother to my children.

We don't expect you to take Gro's place, but we do respect you, and I expect we can have a good life together. You can write me your answer at my cousin Elmer's.

His address is on the envelope.

Sincerely,

Jon Ytterhorn

When they had finished reading the letters the midwife came up to Pa. "Mr. Ytterhorn," she said. "Mrs. Lars Jensen from Bergen just gave birth to a baby boy. He was stillborn. She is grieving for him and would be happy to take your baby and relieve you of the hardship of raising an infant without a mother."

"We'll manage," said Pa.

"It might be difficult travelling without a wet nurse," she said.

"Pa," said Signe. "We can't give up Carrie."

"No," said Pa. "Carrie is our consolation and gives Gro's death meaning. We can't lose her, too."

The midwife left and Signe said, "Wherever we go, there will be mothers nursing babies, and I know they will share with Carrie."

○　○　○

Three days later, Trygve awoke early in the morning and went up on deck and stood at the railing, watching. The horizon looked different this morning. It was like a thin purple cloud stretched all the way across the horizon.

He watched a sailor climb the mast up to the crow's nest. He pointed ahead and yelled, "LAND!" After nine weeks and three days at sea land was in sight.

Trygve went back down to their quarters to share the news with Pa, but he was sleeping. He went back up to the deck and stared ahead, just thinking. Soon they would be in the new land. It didn't cause great excitement for him because life would never be the same without Ma. He thought his dreams had died with her.

There was a ripple of excitement amongst everyone on the ship as they began the day with land in sight. At last! In a few days the long journey across the Atlantic Ocean would be over.

Trygve spent the morning at the railing, waiting and thinking. He thought about his Ma and the other people who had died. They never got to see America.

Signe came and stood by him, and together they watched a steamer speed by their sailing ship. It appeared and was gone again in almost no time at all. "I hear those steamships can cross the ocean in only two weeks," said Signe.

"But they cost as much for just one person as it does for a whole family on a sailing ship," said Trygve.

For the rest of that day the scenery was interesting. Instead of the seemingly endless ocean, they saw a lighthouse, two jagged rocks sticking out of the ocean, islands, fishing boats, and birds that landed on the *Franklin's* deck. But when evening came, the mainland didn't seem much nearer than it had that morning.

Three days later the boat stopped at an island, and a doctor came on board to inspect the immigrants. "Your people look healthier than the last boat I inspected," said the doctor to the captain. "There was an outbreak of diphtheria, and forty-two died at sea."

"We lost eight people including a newborn," said the captain.

The Ytterhorn family stood together as the doctor made his rounds. "You seem like a healthy family," said the doctor. "Where is the baby's mother?"

Pa looked straight ahead and without a shred of emotion said, "She got the childbirth fever and died."

"I am sorry to hear that," said the doctor, and he moved on to the next family.

When the doctor was through with his inspection, he handed the captain a sheet of paper. "These persons will have to remain on the island until they are better," said the doctor.

"I hope none of the Nielsons are on that list," said Pa.

"They're all healthy," said Signe. "And they're going to Milwaukee."

"Elmer says it's best for us to go across the Great Lakes to Milwaukee and then take a train over to Iowa," said Pa. Then he asked, "How are they getting to Lake Huron?"

"They're taking a train," answered Signe.

"I'll ask if they mind if we travel with them," said Pa. "Then we won't have to find another woman to nurse Carrie until Milwaukee."

After the doctor was gone, the captain of a small steam boat came on board. Trygve couldn't hear what he was saying, but it looked like he was arguing with Captain Vigen. After a few minutes, Captain Vigen gave the other captain some money. Then he yelled to the sailors, "Reef the sails, boys."

The young sailors scrambled up the masts and started rolling the sails, and then the captain of the steamboat connected his tow rope to the *Franklin*.

Captain Vigen came by. "You can pack up your things," he said to the expectant passengers who waited to see what would happen next. "We hope to pull into Quebec sometime during the night and unload in the morning."

○  ○  ○

Early the next morning, Pa and Trygve packed their quilts into the trunk and brought it and the box up to the deck. They left the casks down in the hold because they were nearly empty now, just a little oatmeal in the one, and they would cook it up that day. They placed the trunk and the box next to the Nielson's belongings which were heaped on the main deck. They were ready.

There were money-changers on the dock, and the two men exchanged Norwegian kroner for Canadian dollars, just enough to pay for the rail ticket and one dollar each for a little food. Then Pa paid five cents for a loaf of white bread and a flask of fresh milk. He broke the bread into four pieces and he and his children stood in a circle and ate the bread and drank the milk.

Then Pa, Trygve, and Mr. Nielson began carrying their trunks and crates over to the railroad station. When they were carrying the last of their things, Signe carried baby Carrie and followed Trygve and the men. She said to Rolf,

"Hold on to my skirt so we don't get separated." Mrs. Nielson followed Signe carrying her baby, with her children holding on to her skirt.

The men and Trygve hauled their belongings to the train and placed them in the middle of a boxcar. Trygve lifted Rolf up onto the train and then held Carrie while Signe climbed up, and they all sat down on one of the planks that ran along the sides of the boxcar. The Nielsons followed and sat next to them.

Carrie began to cry and Mrs. Nielson and Signe traded babies. Carrie latched on to Mrs. Nielson's breast and was soon satisfied. More trunks and crates were loaded, and three more families crowded into the boxcar.

The train lurched forward, and Trygve's whole family, the Nielson family, and almost everybody else fell on the floor. A crate fell on Trygve. He got up, rubbing his head. They all braced themselves as they waited for the train to move again. Soon it jerked and began to jiggle and move slowly.

The train picked up speed, and soon they were moving very fast, or at least it seemed so to Trygve. He wished he could see the countryside, but he didn't have a good view out of the open door. The clickety-clack of the wheels and the rocking motion of the train made him sleepy. He watched Rolf curl up on the floor and fall asleep. He pulled their America trunk close and draped himself over it and was soon sound asleep. He dreamed of the land they would have and of Ma, too. She was in a splendid house. Then he jerked and woke up as the train screeched to a stop at a station.

They got out, stretched, shared a loaf of bread, and climbed back on the train. Trygve, Pa, and Signe took turns sleeping on the trunk. Twelve hours later the train stopped, and everyone got out. They saw a great body of water.

"It's the ocean," said Rolf.

"No," said Signe. "It's a lake. A big, big lake."

The sun hung low in the sky and glistened on the water, almost blinding Trygve as he tried to see to the other side. He stood by his family's belongings while Pa paid for another fare. He hoped they would have enough money left to get to Cousin Elmer's.

"How long will it take us to get to Milwaukee?" Trygve asked a man who was loading freight.

"Oh, about thirty-six hours."

The immigrants once again hauled their trunks and crates and loaded them onto the steamer. Each family stood by its own belongings. Because of Carrie, the Ytterhorns stayed close to the Nielsons.

"It's going to take us thirty-six hours to get there," announced Trygve.

"Then we better make up some beds here on the floor," said Signe. She opened up the trunk, took out the feather ticks, and spread them on the floor of the steamship next to their things.

Trygve went to the railing and gazed at the amber sun sinking into the water in front of him and the white moon rising up behind him. Soon their great journey would be over. But things weren't the way they were supposed to be.

During the second night on the steamer a wind came up and it began to rain. Pa and Trygve held a feather tick over Rolf and Signe, who held Baby Carrie close to keep her warm. Pa and Trygve got soaked to the skin. Trygve shivered and said, "I hope we don't get sick from this."

"We're tough," said Pa. "We got to be."

The next morning a warm sun came out and dried the immigrants as the steamship pulled into Milwaukee. As the ship pulled into port Mrs. Nielson took baby Carrie and nursed her one more time. "I'd be happy to take her with us," she said.

"That's kind of you," said Pa. "But we have to keep her."

"Goodbye, little one," said Mrs. Nielson. "I hope you don't get too hungry."

"Thank you for helping us," said Pa.

"There was plenty for two babies," said Mrs. Nielson.

After unloading his family's things, Mr. Nielson helped Pa and Trygve carry the trunk and the box to the train station. "Good-bye and good luck," said Mr. Nielson.

"And good luck to you," said Pa. "I hope many good things will come to you and your family."

Trygve stood next to Pa at the train station. Another Norwegian pointed to the money exchanger, and Pa went and exchanged all of his Norwegian kroner for American dollars. Then they headed for the ticket booth.

The ticket agent spoke English. He said to Pa, "Where you going?"

Pa didn't understand him and just shrugged his shoulders. Another man turned to Pa and said in Norwegian, "Where are you heading?"

"To Iowa," said Pa.

"Where in Iowa?" asked the ticket agent. Pa looked at the Norwegian, who continued to interpret for him.

"North of Decorah near Hesper," said Pa.

The Norwegian man spoke English to the ticket agent and then he said to Pa, "Tickets to McGregor, Iowa for one adult and two children come to thirteen dollars and sixty cents. The baby and the little boy ride for free."

Pa counted out the American dollars and after he paid the ticket agent there was only one thin dime left in the palm of his hand. A railroad worker took the America trunk and the box. He made tickets for them and gave the stubs to Pa. Then two other workers loaded them onto a boxcar.

Pa looked at the dime and went out into the street and bought a loaf of bread for the train ride. Then, carrying Rolf in one arm and the large loaf of white bread in the other, he climbed up into one of the train's coaches. Trygve and Signe, who was carrying Carrie, followed Pa. Trygve looked around at the seats and the walls. He had never seen anything so grand. The seats were black leather with red velvet and gold braid trim. He sat down next to Pa and Rolf.

But Signe didn't sit down with them. She sat down across the aisle next to a blonde woman with a baby. Trygve wondered if the lady understood Norwegian.

He listened to her say to the woman, "Missus, this is my baby sister."

"What a pretty little baby," said the lady in Norwegian.

"Our mother died on the sailing ship," said Signe. "She had childbirth fever."

"I'm so sorry," said the woman.

"A lady on the ship nursed her all the way across the ocean and on the steamer, but she stayed in Milwaukee."

"Now who's feeding her?" asked the lady.

"Nobody," said Signe. "I was wondering if you could when she gets hungry?"

"Well," said the lady. "I don't know if I'd have enough for both my baby and yours. I don't think I want to."

Signe looked around the railroad carriage to see if there were any other women with babies but didn't see any.

"How long will it take to get to Iowa?" asked Signe.

"About six hours," replied the lady.

After about an hour, Carrie woke up. Signe rocked her back and forth and put her finger in the baby's mouth so she could suck on it. Carrie settled down for a few minutes, but then she began to cry hard. Everyone in their carriage was looking at Signe and at Carrie, who got louder and louder.

"Okay, I'll feed your baby," said the woman. Signe took the woman's little one and handed Carrie to her. Carrie became quiet and content. Two hours later the woman and her baby got off of the train and Signe started looking around at the women who were boarding. A woman with a one-year-old sat down next to Signe. She spoke to her child in Norwegian.

"How far are you going?" asked Signe.

"To Iowa," answered the woman.

"Could you nurse our baby when she gets hungry?" asked Signe.

"What?" said the woman.

"Can you feed my baby sister when she wakes up?"

"Where's your mother?" asked the woman.

"She died on the sailing ship."

"Oh, that's too bad," said the woman. "I'd be happy to nurse your baby."

As the train drew closer to Iowa, Trygve thought about his Ma. This wasn't the way they had planned it. He didn't even care about getting rich anymore. He wondered how long before Rebekka would get his Pa's letter. Would she come? He hoped not.

The train began to cross a wide river and a man in a black uniform with gold braid came and took the last of Pa's tickets and said in a loud voice, "McGregor, Iowa is the next stop."

Pa, Trygve, Rolf, and Signe, who was still holding Carrie, stood on the train platform next to their America trunk, the box, and Carrie's little bed.

Pa looked at the four pennies he still had. "I wonder if it will buy a loaf of bread."

"I'll go and see," said Trygve and he took the four cents and went into a bakery. When he came out with a loaf of bread, Pa was talking to a man who had a boy about Trygve's age with him.

"Where you from?" asked the man.

"Oksfjord," said Pa. "That's in the far north."

"Yes, I know where it is," said the man. "We came from Tromso."

"We passed by Tromso on the fishing boat," said Trygve.

"My name is Ole Olson, and my son is Alfred," he said, reaching out to shake Pa's hand. "Welcome to America."

"Thank you," said Pa. "I'm Jon Ytterhorn, and these are my children: Trygve, Signe, Rolf and baby Carrie."

"And where are you heading?"

"To start with we're going to my cousin Elmer's near Hesper. That's supposed to be about ten miles north of Decorah."

"How are you getting there?"

**64**

"I guess we'll have to walk."

"Get in my wagon and you can ride the first ten miles," he said as he looked around. Then he asked, "Where's the baby's mother."

"She died on the sailing ship," said Pa. "But we've managed to find women to nurse Baby Carrie, so far."

"When is she due to eat again?"

"Probably in about two hours," said Signe, who was carrying the sleeping baby.

"My wife is still nursing our little boy. If we hurry, we can get there before she's hungry again."

They loaded the trunk and the box onto the wagon and climbed up. Pa sat in front with Mr. Olson, and Alfred sat on the floor with Rolf and let Trygve and Signe have the seat. When they were all settled in, Mr. Olson shook the reins and started the horses at a trot.

"How long have you been in America?" asked Pa.

"It'll soon be ten years, but I haven't farmed the whole time because I had to go to the war. This will just be my second crop since the war."

They rode in silence for about fifteen minutes. Then Mr. Olson said, "There's been a lot of rain this year and we're awfully late at getting the seed in the ground. Do you think you and your son would like to work for me for the rest of this week? Then we could take you up to your cousin's on Sunday. And, besides, I'll pay you each a dollar."

"That is most kind of you," said Pa. "I was worried about how we'd get there."

"And I was worried about Carrie getting enough to eat," said Signe to Trygve.

"You were right, Signe," said Trygve. "People are good. Things are turning out okay." Then he whispered, "Except for Ma."

Signe whispered back, "Except for Ma." Her chin puckered, and tears made rivulets down her dusty cheeks.

Trygve fought back the tears that were welling up in his own eyes. Pa turned around and looked at Signe and Trygve. "Something the matter?" he asked.

"We're remembering Ma," answered Trygve.

"Yes," Pa said, and soon he put his hands over his face. Trygve could tell that Pa was crying.

Rolf looked at his Pa, and Trygve, and Signe and asked, "Why's everybody crying?"

"We're just remembering Ma," said Pa. "I guess we haven't really mourned properly for her since she died."

"A person needs to mourn," said Mr. Olson. They didn't say anything the rest of the way.

Mr. Olson brought his team to a halt in front of a new two-story white house. A robust woman with blonde hair and round, red cheeks came out of the house with a six-year-old hiding behind her skirts.

"This is Mr. Ytterhorn and his children. They just arrived from Oksfjord. Mrs. Ytterhorn died on the sailing ship, and the baby needs to eat."

Mrs. Olson reached for the baby, who was already awake and fussing. "Poor little thing," she said.

"And I thought Mr. Ytterhorn and his boy Trygve could help me get the crop in. Then we could give them a ride up to his cousin's place on Sunday."

"That sounds good," said Mrs. Olson. Then she went and whispered something in Mr. Olson's ear as he climbed down from the wagon.

Mr. Olson looked embarrassed. "My wife is worried about the bedbugs," he said. "Everybody gets them on the ships."

"We got our share of bites," said Pa.

"Alfred," said Mrs. Olson. "Go and get your and your Pa's other sets of clothes for Mr. Ytterhorn and Trygve. I'll get clothes for Signe and Rolf."

Then she looked at Pa and said, "I'll boil up all your clothes and blankets so those varmints can't set up housekeeping with you."

"I'm mighty obliged," said Pa.

They changed clothes in the barn, and when they came out, Carrie wasn't hungry anymore. "I'll cook up some more potatoes," said Mrs. Olson.

*It's June and they still have some of last year's potatoes,* thought Trygve. *And they've got a new house built out of sawed boards.* He wondered how many years they had lived in the log cabin beside the house. Before they even got inside, he could smell a most wonderful aroma.

"We're having rabbit," said Mrs. Olson.

"I caught it in my trap," said Alfred.

When they sat down at the table, there was more food than Trygve had ever seen at one time. There was a big bowl of potatoes, rutabaga, peas and lettuce from the garden, bread and butter, cheese, and a cake with strawberries. It was even more than they had ever had at Grandmother's house. He wished Ma could have seen it.

"This is a lot of food," said Pa.

"Yes," said Mr. Olson. "In Norway we never had enough to eat. Sometimes all we had was oatmeal and fish."

"In Norway, only the rich people have this much food," said Trygve.

"Here, anyone who's willing to work has enough to eat," said Mr. Olson.

After supper, Alfred said to Trygve, "Want to help with chores?"

"Sure," said Trygve.

"If we get done fast enough, maybe we can check my traps."

"That would be fun," said Trygve.

They went into the barn, and Alfred handed Trygve a pail. "You milk that one," he said.

"They sure are different from the goats I've milked," said Trygve.

"But it's the same. They're just bigger," said Alfred.

After chores, they went into the house and Alfred got down the rifle. "It's a muzzle loader," he said. "We use this in the winter to shoot deer and bear. It would be fun to shoot small animals with it, but Pa says the shot is too costly."

The next day Pa scattered the wheat on an already prepared field, and Trygve walked behind the plow in another field. He was careful to make the furrows straight. Mr. Olson walked behind, making a line with a stick, and Alfred made lines in the other direction. "We're trying corn for the first time this year," said Mr. Olson. "It's good feed for the animals and plentiful."

When they were through making lines, Mr. Olson made holes with the hoe where the lines crossed and Alfred dropped two seeds of corn in each hole.

"This sure looks like good dirt," said Trygve.

"Everything grows really fast," said Alfred.

They worked from sunup to sundown and after the third day Mr. Olson said, "I can't believe it. All of my crop is in the ground. I surely do appreciate your good help. We can leave for your cousin's in the morning."

Early the next morning, before the sun had even come up behind the hill, Mr. Olson, Pa, Alfred, and Trygve were in the barn milking the cows. Mr. Olson said, "My brother's boy will help Alfred while we're gone. We all like to help each other out."

"How long will it take to get to Decorah?" asked Pa.

"About a day and a half if we push it," answered Mr. Olson. "Two days if we take it easy."

"You'll be gone three or four days getting us there," said Pa.

"And you and Trygve worked hard for me for three days," said Mr. Olson. "I call it a fair exchange. Besides that it gives us an excuse to visit my cousin."

Pa rode in the front of the wagon with Mr. Olson, while Signe sat in the back next to Mrs. Olson and her little boy, and Trygve and Rolf sat on the floor in the rear with the America trunk and the box. "We'll spend tonight with my cousin," said Mr. Olson. "He has a place near Frankville."

They went down steep hills and around curves. The trees made a canopy over the road, keeping the warm sun away. They passed farms with fields of wheat and corn, and saw many animals.

"Almost all of the houses and barns are new," said Signe.

"That's because this is new country," said Mrs. Olson. "Ten years ago, there weren't very many white people here in Iowa."

"Who was here?" asked Signe.

"Just the Indians."

"Where are they now?"

"The government made them move out west."

It was late afternoon when the wagon pulled into Mr. Olson's cousin's farm. Mr. Olson's cousin came out to meet them. His left leg was gone, and he used a crutch.

"He lost his leg in the war," said Mrs. Olson. "I'm so thankful my Ole came home all in one piece."

Trygve looked around at the large house and the barn with cows in it. He looked at the pigs and sheep in the pens in the barnyard and said to Signe, "Everybody in America is as rich as the Dahls."

"Yes," said Signe. "But they don't act like it."

Mr. Olson's cousin Lars said, "Welcome, welcome! What good fortune brings my cousin to see me?"

"We are taking our guests to his cousin's place up past Decorah."

"There is plenty of room here to spend the night," said Lars Olson. "And my wife will have supper cooked up for you in no time at all."

"You are all so good," said Pa.

"We all remember what it was like to be poor," said Lars. "So poor that we were afraid we might starve."

"That's what makes them different from the Dahls," said Signe to Trygve. "The Dahls never knew what it was like to be poor."

"I hope we don't ever forget," said Trygve.

"Are you going to settle here or go west?" asked Lars.

"We plan to go to the Dakota Territory next spring," answered Pa.

Lars looked around and then asked Pa, "Your wife?"

"She died on the sailing ship," said Pa, looking down at the dirt.

"I'm so sorry," said Lars, and Trygve could tell that he meant it.

The next morning Trygve woke up with the rooster crowing. His Pa and Mr. and Mrs. Olson were already eating breakfast. "We want to get an early start," said Mr. Olson, "If we can make good enough time, we can make it back here for tonight."

As they climbed up into the wagon, Pa said, "Today's the day."

"What day?" asked Trygve.

"The day that we arrive at Uncle Elmer's and our long journey will be over," answered Pa.

"How long has it been?" asked Mr. Olson.

"Eleven weeks and three days," said Pa.

"And our lives have changed forever," whispered Trygve.

"But this is what Ma wanted," said Signe. "And she might have died even if we had stayed."

The wagon moved steadily along the road, down a hill and around a curve, and Trygve became sleepy. He laid down on the floor of the wagon next to the America trunk and fell asleep. He dreamed of a large white house with red shutters. The sign above the door said Ytterhorn. In his dream he walked up the stone walk, and his Ma opened the door and walked towards him.

The wagon stopped, and he woke up. Mr. Olson was asking a man, "Which way to Decorah?"

"Turn left," said the stranger. "You go down a long hill, and you come to the town."

An hour later they were in the town of Decorah. Mr. Olson stopped the horses and asked a group of men who were standing in a circle on a corner, "Does anyone here know where Elmer Ytterhorn lives?"

"He lives just off of the Hesper Road," said one man. "You go north out of town, and it will be the third road on the right."

An hour later they were on the Hesper Road and Mr. Olson stopped the horses again. "Can you tell me where the Elmer Ytterhorn place is?"

"Go to the third crossroad and turn left. It will be the second place on the right."

Trygve sat up straight and looked at the hills and the streams and scrutinized every farm. They would soon be at Uncle Elmer's. They turned off the Hesper road and went by the first place on the right. As they approached the next farm, they watched eagerly. They saw a man and a boy sawing up a tree on the edge of the clearing.

"That's Elmer, and it must be his boy, Sven, with him," said Pa.

"I don't hardly remember them at all," said Trygve.

"You must have been about four years old when they left," said Pa. "I remember how everyone said it was foolishness. And now look at him with his new house and land of his own."

"They said I shouldn't go either," said Mr. Olson. "But it's the best thing I ever did."

Elmer Ytterhorn looked up from his sawing and saw the wagon. Pa stood up and waved his arms, and Elmer came running. He said to Sven, "Go and fetch your Ma and tell her they're here."

Pa jumped from the wagon and ran to his cousin, and they hugged each other. Then Elmer looked up at the wagon for almost a minute with his brow furrowed before he finally asked, "Where's Gro?"

"She got the childbirth fever and died at sea," said Pa. Then he whispered, "The bottom of the ocean is her final resting place."

Elmer held Pa, and they cried together. "She was so beautiful, and so kind, and good," said Elmer.

Mr. Olson shook the reins, and the horses pulled the wagon over to the house. Trygve looked up and saw Pa's cousin and two younger children running towards them.

Gunhild looked at the wagon and then over at Pa and Cousin Elmer. "Gro," she said. "Where's Gro?"

Neither Trygve nor Signe answered her. She looked worried and whispered it again. "Where's Gro?"

Rolf broke the silence. "She in the bottom of the ocean."

"Oh, no," said Gunhild in disbelief. "What happened?"

"She got the childbirth fever and died," said Signe.

Gunhild covered her face with her apron and bawled. "Oh, how I've been looking forward to seeing her. But I best pull myself together and get some lunch for our guests."

"Oh, yes," said Pa. "This is Mr. and Mrs. Olson. They've brought us all the way from McGregor."

"It was good for both of us," said Mr. Olson. "Mr. Ytterhorn and his boy helped me put in my crop."

Mrs. Olson looked at Gunhild and asked, "Will you be able to feed the baby?"

"Oh, yes," said Gunhild. "Little Nels is napping. He's fourteen months now and still nursing. I'm sure there's enough for the little one."

When they were through eating, Mr. Olson shook Pa's hand and said, "I wish you much success, and be sure to stop in if you ever come to McGregor."

Mrs. Olson reached out for Carrie and held her one last time. "Good-bye, little one. Grow up and be strong." Then she handed her back to Signe.

"Thank you," said Signe. "She grew a lot last week."

Pa shook Mrs. Olson's hand and said, "Thank you both for everything. Your kindness has meant a lot to all of us."

"Well, we best be going," said Mr. Olson. "We want to get back to my cousin's before dark."

Although it was the middle of the afternoon, Cousin Elmer sat in the parlor with Pa. They had so much to talk about. Elmer wanted to know everything about life in Oksfjord. Gunhild came into the room and listened intently. Trygve and Svend listened from the dining room.

Trygve heard Gunhild ask, "What about Rebekka? Did she ever marry?"

"No," said Pa. "You remember she was always Gro's best friend. I have written to her and asked her to come to America to marry me and be a mother to my children."

"That would be a good thing if she would come," said Elmer. "It can be hard enough even with a wife, but almost impossible if you have to be both father and mother to your children."

"And Rebekka is a good woman," said Gunhild. "I remember she was always kind to everyone."

"From what I hear, you will need all the help you can get," said Elmer. "Making a home in the Dakota Territory won't be easy."

"And for now it will be good for me to have a woman here to visit with," said Gunhild.

Trygve looked at Svend and whispered, "Let's go. I want to get out of here."

They went outside and Svend said to Trygve, "It bothers you when your Pa talks about getting married to Rebekka, doesn't it?"

"Yes," said Trygve. "Nobody can ever take the place of my Ma."

"I'm sure of that," said Svend with sympathy, and the boys stood quietly, watching Signe, who held Carrie, and Mari, who was about a year older than Signe and was watching baby Nels toddle around the yard. They watched Rolf and five-year-old Bjorn play in a pile of straw.

Then Trygve said, "Let's go."

"What do you want to see?" asked Svend.

"Everything," said Trygve. "All of your animals, your fields, the woods, and whatever else."

They walked through a field of sprouting wheat. Trygve reached down and picked up a fistful of the black loam, rubbed it, and let it sift through his fingers. "The dirt is so rich here. I bet almost anything would grow in it."

"My Pa says it's ten times better than the soil in Oksfjord," said Svend.

They stopped at a stream. "I see a fish," said Trygve.

"There's trout in this here stream," said Svend. "We can go fishing tonight after the chores are done, if you like."

○ ○ ○

At the supper table that night Cousin Elmer said, "Jon, I know you want to start earning money right away. There is plenty of work in Decorah. I hear they need carpenters for a hotel, and I also heard they need men for building the railroad."

"I'll look into it tomorrow," said Pa.

"And there's a farmer down the road who sells milk in Decorah and is milking more than twenty cows. He's asked me about letting Svend help, but right now he's my right hand man. I bet he could use Trygve until school starts up again."

"I'd like that," said Trygve.

"The two of you together could earn enough to get a good start next spring," said Elmer. "Do you plan to buy here or go west?"

"I think we'll go to the Dakota Territory," said Pa. "When's the earliest we'll be able to leave?"

"April," answered Elmer.

Trygve counted on his fingers. "That's nine months to get ready," he said.

"Nine months to work, go to school, and learn English," said Gunhild.

"I can help you learn English," said Mari.

"Good idea," said Gunhild. "Every night after chores, we can have English lessons."

○   ○   ○

Five weeks and one day after Jon Ytterhorn and his family had arrived, the letter from Rebekka came in the mail. He read it at the supper table.

Dear Jon,

I received your letter last week and mourn for you and your children and for Gro's mother and sisters. Although I probably never would have seen her again, knowing that she is no longer of this world is most grievous to me.

For days I have struggled with my response to your letter and asked myself serious questions. I want to know how best can I live out my life so that this poor world will be a better place because I have lived on it. It seems that the answer is for me to come to America and do as you have asked of me. Although I know that I can never take Gro's place I pray that I might be a worthy wife and mother to your children.

My parents give me their blessings and have purchased a ticket on a steam ship that will take me to New York. From there I will travel by train and hope to arrive there on the eighteenth day of August at McGregor, Iowa.

Yours respectfully,

Rebekka Thorson

"August eighteenth," said Pa. "That's coming up real soon." Pa and Elmer got up from the table and walked over to the calendar.

"It's the day after tomorrow," said Elmer.

"That means I have to leave for McGregor tomorrow," said Pa. "It is so soon, and we are getting along fine here."

"Without her," finished Trygve.

Pa looked at Trygve, who was looking down at the floor, and said, "Trygve I know that you have your mind made up not to like Rebekka, but I want you to remember one thing. I have asked Rebekka to come to America. She is leaving her family and Oksfjord behind. She may end up lonesome and homesick and I want for all of us, including you, to help her feel welcome."

Trygve looked up, "Yes, Pa. I'll try," he said. "I understand that we'll need a woman when we go west. I just wish she wasn't coming now."

"But she is," said Pa.

"And you all will need someone to cook, and sew, and keep the house," said Elmer. "Even if you could get everything done, it takes a woman to make a home."

"Yes," said Pa. "When we leave here, we will need a woman in our home."

"I still wish she wasn't coming," said Trygve. "She'll never take Ma's place."

"No, she won't," said Pa. "Especially for you and Signe. But when we go west, you and I will toil from sun up to sun down, and Rolf and Carrie will need a mother."

Pa looked at Signe and asked, "How do you feel about Rebekka?"

"She won't be the same as Ma," said Signe. "But maybe she'll be someone to comfort me when I'm missing Ma. And she'll be someone for me to talk to. I remember she used to take time to talk to me after church." Trygve remembered how she always talked to them. She had been different than other grownups, but she would never be his Ma.

It was late on Saturday night when the wagon pulled into the yard. Trygve sat up in bed with his head next to the window and heard his Pa say in a soft voice, "Rebekka, we're here now."

"Oh, I must have fallen asleep," she answered.

"Let me help you down," said Pa.

Trygve heard Cousin Elmer and Gunhild go down the steps and out into the yard. "Welcome to America," said Gunhild. "You must be very tired and hungry, too."

Cousin Elmer helped Pa carry Rebekka's trunk inside, and the four adults went into the kitchen. Trygve went into the hallway and sat by the register that was just above the kitchen. Signe came out of her room and sat next to him. She pulled her knees up under her nightgown and when she leaned forward her long hair fell around her face and shoulders. She reminded him of Ma. They watched Gunhild slice the bread and cheese and dish up applesauce.

"What a grand place you have here," said Rebekka.

"In a few years you will have a good house, too," said Gunhild. "We lived in the log cabin for five years."

Trygve and Signe grew sleepy as they listened to the latest news from Oksfjord but became wide awake when they heard Elmer ask, "When do you plan to marry?"

"Not right away," said Pa. "Rebekka thinks we all need more time to grieve for Gro."

"Lots of time," whispered Trygve.

"And we need to get to know each other better," said Rebekka. "Maybe we'll be ready by Christmas."

"I think that is wise," said Gunhild. "We better get to bed now because morning comes soon. For now Rebekka can sleep in with the girls." She started putting the dishes in the dish pan.

"Let me wash these," said Rebekka.

"No," said Gunhild. "They can wait till morning."

Trygve and Signe watched the grownups arise from the table and they quickly tiptoed back to their beds.

At the breakfast table the next morning, Trygve was silent. He watched Rebekka. Her brown hair was pulled back into a bun. He compared her with his Ma. Ma had blonde hair and was quite a bit prettier. He had heard that she was the prettiest girl in her school. Rebekka was wearing a blue calico dress with a white apron over it, but even with that nice dress, she was plain looking.

When Gunhild was through nursing Carrie, she handed her to Rebekka. "What a pretty baby," said Rebekka. "I do believe she looks just like Gro."

"She does," said Gunhild.

"Precious little darling," said Rebekka. "Your Ma will live on in you."

"I like that," said Signe. "Our Ma sort of comes alive again in baby Carrie."

Rebekka held Carrie's cheek next to her own and softly hummed a tune to her. Soon Carrie was asleep, and Rebekka placed her in the new cradle that Pa had made.

When the chores were finished, the two families dressed for church. So far, Trygve had not gone to church because he had never been through with chores at the dairy farm where he milked cows every morning and evening. He had been happy for the excuse because he didn't want to have anything to do with God, certainly not the God who had taken his mother away from him. But he was through working at the dairy farm and knew better than to try and stay home.

The eleven Ytterhorns and Rebekka climbed into the wagon, and Trygve inspected the farms as they rolled past. Large houses, small houses, big barns painted red, and corn that was as high as the wagon. They stopped at the school in Hesper. "I thought we were going to church," said Trygve.

"We are," said Gunhild. "But we meet at the school because we haven't built a church building yet."

"We've only been a congregation for two years," said Elmer.

"Pastor Stub isn't anything like Pastor Johanson," said Signe. "He doesn't shout or bang his fists."

"Is he as long-winded?" asked Trygve.

"He talks for about an hour," said Pa.

Once the service started Trygve listened briefly, but Pastor Stub's droning voice soon had Trygve nodding. Pa poked him with his elbow, and he sat up straight and started daydreaming of the place they would have in the Dakota territory. But his vision had an empty spot and he couldn't put Rebekka into it. He told himself it didn't really matter without his Ma.

After dinner, Rebekka went upstairs to her trunk and brought down a small satchel and set it on the table. "I brought some gifts for the children," she said.

She opened it and took out two very small brown cloth sacks with drawstrings at the top. "Penknives for Trygve and Svend." She reached back into the satchel and brought out two small white boxes and handed them to to Signe and Mari.

Signe opened hers carefully. "It's beautiful," she said, looking at the silver brooch with small blue stones on it. Mari's brooch was identical to Signe's except it had pink stones.

She brought out two more boxes from her satchel and handed them to Rolf and Bjorn, who were delighted with the gifts of wooden soldiers.

As the children stood around her, Rebekka pulled the satchel wide open and pointed to the bottom. Then she lifted out the box with the creamer, sugar bowl, and four cups and saucers. "I bought these at your auction. I wanted something to remember your Ma by. When I came to visit her, we drank coffee from these cups. When we have our house in the Dakota Territory we will drink coffee from them and remember your Ma."

Signe held a cup as though it were a precious thing. Trygve said, "I will like that." After a moment he said, "Thank you," and then went outside.

Svend followed him and said, "That was sure swell of Rebekka to bring us gifts."

"Yes," said Trygve. "But I hope she doesn't think she can buy my affection."

"She's trying hard to be kind," said Svend. "I think you should give her a chance."

○ ○ ○

On the first Sunday in December, Trygve overheard Pa talking with Pastor Stub after the Sunday service. "I'm wondering if you could do a wedding service for me and Rebekka Thorson."

"What do you have in mind?" asked Pastor Stub.

"A short ceremony at my cousin's house after church next Sunday," said Pa.

"Yes," said Pastor Stub. "I can come then."

On the way home Trygve watched Rebekka, who was holding Carrie in one arm and had her other arm around Rolf. He whispered to Signe, "I bet Rolf is already forgetting our Ma."

"Perhaps," said Signe. "But we won't, and I'm sure Pa won't."

"We certainly won't," said Trygve, scowling at Rebekka.

"I wish you wouldn't feel that way," said Signe. "Ma is gone, and we can't get her back, and I am glad Pa sent for Rebekka. She is so kind to all of us."

"I'm not glad she's here," said Trygve. "But you're right. She is kind. Very kind." But he felt like he was betraying his Ma by saying that Rebekka was kind.

"I bet Ma is looking down at Rebekka holding Carrie and Rolf and smiling," said Signe. "She would have wanted it this way."

Trygve felt out of sorts all week. He didn't like moving his and Svend's beds into Rolf and Bjorn's room so Pa could share their room with Rebekka. He didn't like the baking, sewing, and wedding preparations.

"I don't like all this fuss," he said to Signe.

"A wedding is a joyous occasion," she replied.

"Even when it's just to take someone else's place?" said Trygve.

"Every woman should have a nice wedding," said Signe. "And I know she loves Pa and us, even you."

"She's good and kind, but she couldn't love me."

"Why not?" asked Signe.

"I haven't done anything to deserve it," answered Trygve.

"You will," said Signe. "And even if you don't, she'll probably love you anyway."

○ ○ ○

Sunday afternoon came too soon for Trygve. He watched his Pa standing next to Rebekka. Rebekka looked up at

Pa, and he smiled. *He's forgotten all about Ma*, thought Trygve.

During the first week of April, the last of the snow melted away, and the frost came out of the ground, leaving the road a soft mush. "It's a good thing we got this load of boards here while the road was still frozen," said Pa.

"Yes, Pa," said Trygve, who was unloading boards for the wagon they were building.

"We'll build a good wagon to get us to the Dakota Territory," said Pa.

"I wonder what our life will be like out there," said Trygve.

"We don't know yet," said Pa. "I just know that the land is almost free."

"But at what cost?" said Trygve. "I've heard about people living in houses made of dirt, and Indians killing the settlers."

"There have been Indian problems," said Pa. "But the government has sent soldiers to protect the settlers."

"Is it good land?" said Trygve. "Will we be prosperous like Elmer?"

"I have heard that the soil is rich," said Pa. "It just opened up for settlers in the last year, and I'm hoping to get a choice piece of land."

By the end of the week, the pile of supplies in the shed had grown. Trygve pounded the last nail into the cage he was making.

"What's that?" asked Signe.

"It's for my chickens," said Trygve. "Mr. Ruud from the dairy farm is paying me this week with six chickens so we'll have eggs for the trip."

"Are they going to ride in the wagon?"

"No," said Trygve. "They'll hang on the side."

"It's really going to be loaded," said Signe. "With Pa's tools and Ma's spinning wheel, and Rebekka's pots and pans and dishes, the bags of wheat and meal, and the stove, and the plow. There'll hardly be room for all of us."

"Oh yes," said Pa, who was listening to them. "We'll pack all that on the bottom and put boards over it with the beds on top. Then we'll set the cover on it." He pointed to the white canvas topper sitting on the hay rack in the barn.

"When do we leave?" asked Signe.

"As soon as Carrie learns how to drink from a cup," answered Pa. "Maybe sometime next week."

In the following week, Carrie sat in Rebekka's lap at the supper table and ate mashed potatoes and drank a whole cup of milk. "Good girl," said Pa. "Now we can leave as soon as it stops raining."

The next day Trygve and Signe sat out on the front porch and watched the sun's rays break through the clouds. "I bet tomorrow's the day," said Trygve.

"I'm scared," said Signe.

"Of what?" asked Trygve.

"I don't know," said Signe. "I'm afraid of what I don't know."

"The unknown is scary," said Trygve. "But I am looking forward to having our own place. Uncle Elmer and Aunt Gunhild and everybody else here have been really nice to us but this is their place."

"I wish we could just settle some place around here," said Signe.

"Pa says he could never get a hundred and sixty acres here," said Trygve. "He says Dakota Territory is his land of opportunity."

Pa came outside and said, "Trygve, give me a hand. We're going to load that wagon because tomorrow we roll."

○  ○  ○

The next morning when they pulled out of the yard the sky was clear and the air was cold. Rebekka and Gunhild cried as they said their good-byes. So did Signe and Mari, but the men's and boy's faces were unmoving so as not to show any emotion or fear.

Thus the wagon pulled out of Elmer Ytterhorn's yard with Rebekka sitting next to Pa with a blanket pulled around herself and Carrie. Signe and Rolf sat behind them, and Trygve walked beside the wagon next to their cow, whom they had named Viola, and four sheep. He wanted to make sure they could keep the same pace as the oxen. When he knew the animals could keep up, he tied Viola's rope to the back of the wagon and the sheeps' rope to the side, and he climbed up next to Signe.

A horse-drawn wagon passed them and soon disappeared around a curve in the road. "I wish we had horses instead of oxen," said Signe. "They just lumber along."

"Would be nice," said Trygve. "But we'd have to buy oats for them, and besides oats costing money there will be times when there'll be no oats to buy. Anyway, Viola and the sheep could never keep up with horses."

"It's going to take forever," said Signe.

"About three or four weeks," answered Trygve.

○   ○   ○

The third day after leaving Iowa was cold, wet, and dreary. The oxen plodded forward as the wagon skidded over the rutted trail. Pa sat back under the canvas, trying to keep dry as he watched the oxen.

Rebekka snuggled under a feather tick with Carrie and Rolf and entertained them with the story of Peter and the Wolf.

Trygve and Signe sat in the back of the wagon with the English speller that Aunt Gunhild had given them. Signe called out the words, and Trygve tried to spell them. Rebekka and Pa tried, too. Then Trygve took his turn at calling out the words, but soon no one was answering him except for Pa, as the jiggling of the wagon had rocked them all to sleep.

Soon Trygve was asleep, too, and woke up when he heard his Pa yell, "Whoa!" to the oxen. Then he announced to his waking family, "I think we'll stay here for the night."

Trygve picked up the flap and looked outside at the sopping countryside and said, "I'm glad I brought some dry kindling for our fire in case it rained."

"Good thinking," said Rebekka.

Trygve jumped down from the wagon and was helping Pa remove the yoke from the oxen when he heard a voice. A man driving a cart pulled by mules asked in Norwegian, "Where might you be from and where are you going?"

"We're from Oxfjord," answered Pa. "That's north of Bode, and we're headed for the Dakota Territory."

The man reached out his hand and said, "I'm Herman Soland. We came from down by Christianson four years ago." He spoke a different dialect of Norwegian, but they had no trouble understanding him. Then he said, "It is going to be a miserable night. Why don't you folks come and stay with us. We have a large log cabin and room for everyone."

"That would be so nice," said Rebekka before Pa could protest. Trygve was glad she spoke up because Pa was proud and never wanted to be a bother to anyone.

"It will be such a treat for us to have company. We don't get to do much visiting out here."

"It will be a good night to be sleeping inside," said Pa. He and Trygve put the yoke back on the oxen, and they followed Herman Soland to his log house.

When they got to the house, Herman called out, "Lena, we have company."

Lena came outside and said, "Welcome. Welcome to our humble home. We are so happy to have company. I have not spoken to another woman for more than two weeks."

Quickly the Ytterhorn family went into the Soland's cabin. There was a fire in the stove, and the smell of a roast pork came from the oven. "I'll just peel a few more potatoes, and there will be plenty for everyone."

Three blond heads looked over the side of the loft. "Come down and meet our company," said Lena.

Rebekka picked up a knife and helped Lena peel the potatoes. "I am so grateful that we don't have to try to cook a meal outside tonight."

"Me, too," said Trygve.

After supper, Rebekka helped Lena with the dishes. Then Lena insisted on making a batch of oatmeal cookies for them to take in their wagon. After everyone sampled the cookies, Rebekka helped Lena put down pallets on the floor for the family to sleep on.

The next morning the sun was shining and the Ytterhorns thanked the Solands for the warm night, supper and breakfast, and their good company.

○　○　○

The tenth day of their journey started off the same as all of the others. Trygve woke up when the warm rays of the sun began to heat up the inside of their covered wagon.

He crawled out of his bed to the back of the wagon, untied the flap, and jumped down.

He took the basket of dry kindling from under the wagon. With his jackknife he began peeling a dry, thin branch. Rolf jumped down from the wagon and ran to gather more dead branches from under the trees along the road.

Trygve made a pile of thin shavings, and then he took the flintstone out of his pocket and began striking it with a piece of metal, making sparks. The sparks fell on the shavings. Finally, a spark caught, and a tiny red eye appeared. Trygve blew on it ever so gently, and soon a spiral of smoke appeared. Carefully he added tiny twigs to the shavings and blew on it some more. "Hurry, Rolf," he called. Rolf came running with an armful of twigs and branches and went back into the woods to gather larger twigs and branches.

After he made the fire, he went to a nearby stream to get a pail of water. When he returned, Rebekka began to make the cornmeal mush, and Trygve milked the cow.

"Cornmeal mush," said Signe. "That's something we never had in Norway."

"Just oatmeal," said Pa. "And we were lucky to have that."

When they were through eating breakfast, Rebekka skimmed the cream off the previous night's milk and put it in the butter churn. By noon the jiggling of the wagon had turned it into a nice round ball of butter, and they traded it at a store for a loaf of bread. Then they stopped to water and rest the animals. While the animals grazed, the family ate the bread with yesterday's butter and drank that morning's milk.

Signe and Rolf picked armfuls of flowers, and Trygve took the muzzle loader gun and the fishing pole he had made from a willow branch. "I'm going to catch our supper," he said as he headed for a lake.

Soon he had two nice fish, so he left his line in the water, he loaded the gun, and went to look for rabbits or squirrels. He shot two squirrels and went back to his line, which had another fish on it. He ran back to the wagon and said, "Good eating tonight."

Soon they were moving again. Trygve and Signe sat up front with Pa and Rebekka lay in the back with Carrie and Rolf.

"What's that awful noise?" said Signe.

"Don't know," said Pa.

The squealing became louder and louder. Soon three two-wheel ox carts met them. They were strung together, heavily loaded, driven by one driver and pulled by four of the biggest oxen that Trygve had ever seen.

Pa stopped their covered wagon by the side of the road and asked, "Where will this road take us?"

"You'll come to a fork in the road," said the driver. "The south fork goes all the way to Fort Abercrombie and the north fork goes up to Canada."

"Is Fort Abercrombie in Dakota Territory?" Pa asked.

"Yes," said the man, and they continued on their way.

Trygve leaned against the backboard of the wagon seat and basked in the warm sun. His eyelids became heavy, and he dozed until he heard Signe say.

"Look at that cloud."

Trygve looked at the long gray cloud that stretched across the horizon. "It reminds me of the cloud we saw before that storm we had on the ocean."

As the cloud approached, the air grew cooler. "I think we better stop here by this stream and get water and cook our food," said Pa. "You never know, it could be a big storm."

They worked quickly. Rolf gathered kindling and wood for the fire that Trygve was making. Signe held Carrie while Rebekka cooked the fish and the squirrel.

"If it's raining in the morning it might be hard to get a fire, so I'll cook some oatmeal, too," she said. "And I'll boil up these eggs and make some corn bread."

Trygve milked Viola and set the pail of milk up on the wagon seat. Then he helped Pa tie the animals to a tree next to the wagon.

They ate in silence as the menacing cloud approached. Before they had finished eating, there was a rush of wind and cold rain started pounding them. They quickly picked up the food and dishes, climbed up into the covered wagon, and closed the flaps.

Trygve peeked outside. "It's snowing," he announced.

"It's supposed to be spring," said Signe.

"It can't last too long," said Pa. "Or get too cold."

"We'll just have to bundle together under these quilts and wait for morning," said Rebekka.

"Our body heat should keep us warm," said Pa. He was on one side of her and Trygve on the other.

They listened to wolves howling nearby and the wind rocking their wagon back and forth. Snow blew through the flaps by Trygve's head and it felt like his breath was freezing on the pillow by his face. He slid down further under the thick feather ticks with Rolf in his arms and partly on top of him. His body was now warmed by Rolf's and Signe's, and he drifted off to sleep.

Hours later Trygve woke up. The wind was deafening and a drift of snow half covered him. Through the first rays of dawn, he could make out where the snow was getting in and he pushed most of it off of the quilts and back outside. Then he crawled up on his hands and knees and started to pack what was left against the sides of the loose flap.

Pa looked at him and said, "That's better," and he started pressing the snow around the front flap to ward off the drift that had formed in the front of the wagon.

Signe woke up with fear in her eyes. "We didn't come this far just to die," she said.

"No," said Pa. "We will stay warm under these quilts." Then they all heard it. The canvas that covered their wagon was slowly ripping in the wind. Suddenly there was terror in the covered wagon.

"Oh, Lord have mercy," said Rebekka.

Signe prayed, "God in heaven have mercy on our souls."

Trygve remembered the chorus of voices on the night of the great storm at sea. His Ma had said that God had heard the prayers of His people. He wondered if God was really real, and if he was real was he listening? Just in case, Trygve whispered softly, "God in heaven, have mercy on our souls."

As their prayers raced heavenward, the winds let up, and Rebekka sat up and crawled to the back of the wagon. She pulled up the corner of the mattress and dragged her sewing box out. She took out her largest needle and threaded it with heavy thread. "Pa," she said. "You and me, we're going to sew this thing up."

Pa climbed out and stood on the outside of the wagon leaning over the hole, and Rebekka got up on her knees and pushed the needle through to Pa. He pulled it from the outside and pushed it back to Rebekka. Back and forth they went until soon the canvas was tight and the snow was on the outside.

As Trygve watched Rebekka pull the thread tight and push the needle back through to Pa, he had to admit that she made life a lot easier for their family and it was a good thing she was their new Ma. But admitting that Rebekka was good made him feel like he was betraying his Ma.

When Pa crawled back inside, he was coated with snow. He brushed the thick snow from his hair, his beard, and his face and took off his coat and shook the snow from it. "I think we should try and go back to sleep," he said. "This storm should let up soon, and then we can eat and take care of the animals."

Rebekka reached up to the front seat and poured a cup of last night's milk for Carrie, who was thirsty and drank it quickly. Then they crawled back under the quilts and tried to go back to sleep.

Trygve dozed off, and when he awoke the sky was very bright, but the snow was swirling around their wagon, making deep drifts. He jumped out of the wagon where the animals were huddled together eating snow. Pa climbed down and handed Trygve the milk pail. He quickly began to milk Viola.

"Looks like we'll have to feed the animals some seed," said Pa, looking at the snow-covered ground.

"How long do you think it will take for this to melt?" asked Trygve.

"A day or two," said Pa, as he pulled a bag of corn from the wagon. "Someone told me that corn might not be a good crop in Dakota, anyway."

After feeding the animals, Pa and Trygve climbed back inside. "It's a good thing I cooked up this food last night," said Rebekka as she dished up the oatmeal and corn bread that she had made as the storm was approaching.

They ate quickly. "I'm so cold," said Signe.

"Me, too," said Rolf, shivering.

"Eat fast," said Rebekka. "Then you can get back under the covers."

Soon the Ytterhorn family was once again under the quilts. "There's nothing to do," said Rolf.

"Let's make up some stories," said Rebekka.

"What about?" asked Rolf.

"What do you want them to be about?" asked Rebekka.

"Tell us about when you and Ma got lost in the snow storm on the way home from school," said Signe.

"I've already told you that one three times since we left Iowa."

"How about the time when Pa rescued those two boys in the fjord?" said Trygve.

"I've already told you that one twice," said Pa. "I think Trygve should tell us about when he climbed up the silo and brought down the little Ruud boy."

"How do you know about that?" asked Trygve.

"Mr. Ruud told me. He said if you hadn't gone up and got him, he might have fallen to his death."

"That was brave of you," said Rebekka.

"Not really," said Trygve. "I was milking a cow, and I heard him crying up there, so I just went up and got him down."

"It still took courage," said Rebekka.

Then they heard a voice calling from outside. "Is there anybody in there?" Pa got up and stuck his head outside. Then the voice asked, "Are you alright?"

"We're a little cold, but we're okay," said Pa.

Trygve looked outside and saw the form of a man on a horse outlined in the whirling snow. "We live just down the road," shouted the man. "Come to our house and warm up."

Trygve and Pa jumped down from the wagon and together they hitched the oxen to the wagon and tied Viola and the sheep to the back of the wagon.

Slowly the oxen plowed through the drifted snow behind the man on the horse. After what seemed like at least an hour, they came to a small log cabin.

Pa stopped the oxen in front of it and jumped to the ground, and Rebekka handed Carrie down to him. They all got down and followed the man inside. It was a one room cabin, and the Ytterhorns filled it up.

"That's a mean storm you folks got caught in," said the man. Then he reached out his hand to Pa and said, "I'm Alfred Jensen. Welcome to our home." All of the Ytterhorn family crowded around the stove.

"I'm Jon Ytterhorn," said Pa, rubbing his hands together. "And it sure feels good to get warm."

"These folks spent the night in their wagon," said Mr. Jensen to his wife. "When I saw their wagon, I was afraid that they might be froze to death."

"We're mighty thankful to be alive," said Rebekka.

"Well, you all will just have to stay with us until this snow melts," said Mrs. Jensen. She was obviously glad to have company.

"And I suspect the first thing we need to do is to get your animals some hay," said Mr. Jensen.

"That is so kind of you," said Pa.

"Out here on the frontier, we all help each other," said Mr. Jensen. "When I was coming out here and had problems, a kind family helped us. When I said I can't pay you, the man said 'you won't pay me back, but you'll pay someone else who's in need.' That's the way it works."

"It's like we're all links in a chain," said Pa. "I will remember your acts of kindness when someone comes to me in need."

Two days later the snow had melted enough so that the animals could feed. "Looks like we can be on our way," said Pa.

"You're welcome to stay another day until it's warmer and dryer," said Mr. Jensen.

"I'm much obliged," said Pa. "We sure do appreciate everything you've done for us but we'd like to be on our way."

"I understand," said Mr. Jensen as he followed Pa and Trygve outside.

"How much farther do you think it is to Dakota?" asked Pa.

"With the oxen," said Mr. Jensen, scratching his head, "I'd reckon about another week or so."

Rebekka climbed up into the wagon and Signe handed her baby Carrie before she climbed up, followed by Rolf and Trygve. Pa shook Mr. Jensen's hand and said,

"Thanks again for everything." Then he climbed up and tapped the oxen on their backs with the whip and said, "Come up, now," and the covered wagon was on its way west again.

"It's good to be back in our wagon," said Rebekka.

"Ah, yes," said Pa.

"I don't mean to sound like I'm not grateful for the Jensens taking us in," said Rebekka. "But I felt so crowded in that little cabin I thought I would suffocate."

"We were taking up their space," said Pa. "But soon we'll have our own place."

It was four weeks and three days after leaving Iowa that the Ytterhorn wagon pulled into what had once been the frontier town of Breckenridge on the western edge of Minnesota. There were burned out houses lining the streets.

Trygve looked at a fireplace and chimney that stood as a monument to a home that was now gone. It stood alongside another skeleton of a house with weeds growing where there once was a floor. "I wonder when this house burned down," he said.

"It was probably six years ago when there was an Indian massacre," said Pa. "There weren't enough soldiers to protect the towns because they were all down south fighting the war."

They passed by a sawmill and two houses that were being rebuilt. Pa stopped the wagon and asked the man, "Could you tell me which way to Dakota?"

"It's across that river," said a man, pointing at a fast-moving river. "If you go north for about ten miles you'll come to a ferry that'll get you to the other side."

"Thank you," said Pa.

"We're almost there," said Trygve. "When will we get to our land?"

"Tomorrow or the next day," answered Pa.

"I'm so anxious," said Trygve. "I can't sit still." He jumped down from the wagon and walked alongside. He looked up at the heavily loaded wagon and Rebekka sitting up next to his Pa. It was as if she belonged there, as if she had always been there and everybody had already forgotten about Ma. Tears welled up in his eyes and he thought, *Ma should be up there next to Pa. This was her dream, too.*

After a while Signe climbed down and walked along beside him. "Is something the matter?" she asked.

"Just thinking about Ma," said Trygve. "I wish she was here."

"Me, too," said Signe. They walked on quietly, just thinking of what might have been.

The road ran close to the river and was muddy. In one place the water covered the road, but they kept going. The oxen slowly inched their way through the running water and the wagon sank deeper and deeper into the mud. Finally the oxen stopped.

"Looks like we're stuck." said Pa. "Maybe if everybody gets out it will make a difference."

Rolf and Rebekka with Carrie climbed down and stood next to Trygve and Signe. It didn't make any difference at all. Then Pa jumped down and yelled, "Come up." The oxen pulled and strained but nothing happened.

"It looks like we're going to have to unload this wagon," said Pa, climbing back up on top. He rolled up the feather ticks and dropped them down to Trygve, who handed them to Signe, who handed them to Rebekka, who put them on the grassy bank.

"Rolf, you will have to watch Carrie," said Rebekka. While Rolf watched Carrie the others unloaded the wagon, one piece at a time.

Half an hour later, when the wagon was almost unloaded, Rolf yelled, "Carrie!"

Trygve looked up. They were downstream and Carrie was in the water. He leaped from the wagon and ran jumping over rocks and dead trees, and pulled her from the water. Rebekka was close behind him. She had a look of horror on her face and cried out, "Baby Carrie! Oh, baby Carrie!"

Trygve put Carrie over his knee and slapped her back. Water spurted from her mouth, and she began to cry. "It's okay," said Trygve. "She's just scared."

Rebekka took the sopping baby into her arms. "Thank God," she said. "This family couldn't stand another tragedy."

"No, we couldn't," said Pa, and he walked back to the wagon. Soon he had the much lighter wagon moving out of the mud. When he finally had it up on higher ground he said, "We may as well spend the night here."

Trygve began to gather rocks to make the fire ring. "I'll do the fire," said Pa. "You catch us some supper. Then you can help me load this wagon again."

Trygve took his fishing pole and the muzzle loader and walked down the road into the woods. He was deep in thought when Signe caught up with him.

"You sure have been moody lately," she said.

"I just can't stop thinking about Ma," he said. "Rebekka is kind and good, but I just can't accept her."

"Life would surely be a lot harder without her," said Signe.

"Yes, but..." said Trygve.

"But what?" asked Signe.

"She's not Ma," said Trygve. "Sometimes I catch myself appreciating all the good things she does for us and admiring the way she does things. Then I feel guilty."

"You don't need to," said Signe. "If Ma had known she was going to die, I think she would have chosen this. It's like Ma sent Rebekka to us. I wish for Ma, too. But since we can't ever have her back, I'm glad we have Rebekka."

Trygve's brooding was interrupted by a covey of grouse on the road ahead of them. He lifted his gun and shot three of them. He ran and picked them up and they walked back to their campsite.

"I could have shot ten of them," he said. "But we can only use three."

"That's right," said Pa. "No need to kill what we can't eat. Anyway, it would be wasting shot."

The next morning they pulled into a large settlement. There were many stores and businesses lining the street. They passed by three saloons and a large tent with loud music pouring out of it. Trygve got down and peeked inside and saw a man cranking the handle of a hurdy gurdy and a woman dancing to the music. He wanted to go inside, but right away Pa yelled, "Stay on the sidewalk."

"There's a few things we need," said Pa, stopping the covered wagon in front of a store. A sign over it said "McCauleyville Mercantile." Next to it was a grocery store. They climbed down from the wagon and went into the grocery store.

"I think I'll get another bag of wheat," said Pa. "If we don't use it for planting, we can always grind it for flour."

Rebekka said, "I will see if I can swap this butter for some bread."

While they were in the store, Trygve walked the length of the boardwalk and came to a hotel, a building that said "U. S. Government", and four more saloons. At the end of the street was a sawmill, and on the river side of the road was a boat factory. He looked to the west and at the end of a road he saw a large raft with ropes tied to trees on both the Minnesota side and the Dakota Territory side, and he started to run back to the wagon.

Pa and Rebekka were standing by the wagon. "I bought a barrel of flour," said Rebekka. "It cost ten dollars and coffee and sugar are twenty cents a pound. Everything is so much higher out here."

"They have to ship it farther," said Pa.

"I'll just buy a couple of pounds of coffee," she said. "And we'll use it sparingly." Then she went back inside the store. When she came back out she also had a jug of vinegar, a jug of molasses, and some raisins.

When they were through making their purchases, they piled everything on the back of the wagon and Trygve said, "I found it."

"You found what?" asked Signe.

"I found the ferry," said Trygve, pointing. "It's just down that road." Pa and Rebekka, who was carrying Carrie, climbed up on top of the wagon while Trygve and Signe ran ahead.

There were two soldiers manning the ferry, and when they saw the covered wagon coming down the road, they pulled on the ropes and connected the large raft to the platform on the shore. Then Pa drove the wagon down to the landing, and slowly the oxen pulled the covered wagon onto the ferry.

"You going homesteading?" asked one of the soldiers.

"We're hoping to," said Pa.

"There's plenty of good land out there, and not very much is spoken for yet," said another soldier. "I hope there's still some available when I'm done in the army."

"What about Indians?" asked Trygve.

"About six years ago there was an awful massacre in Breckenridge, and they scalped a lot of white people and burned their houses down," replied the soldier. "But lately they've been pretty quiet."

"Most of them have gone west," said the first soldier. "They shouldn't be any problem."

"How does a person get a homestead?" asked Pa.

"It's not surveyed yet so you just go squat on it."

"What?" asked Pa.

"It's called "Squatter's Rights," said the second soldier.

The first soldier said, "It means you find a quarter of land, that's one hundred and sixty acres, that you like and mark it with stakes. You build a house on it, and plant a crop and live on it for five years and then when it gets surveyed, it will belong to you."

"Or you can get a pre-emption claim," said the second soldier. "You can pay a dollar and a quarter for each acre, and you don't have to live on it."

"And you can also get a tree claim, that's a quarter of land for doing nothing except planting trees on the prairie."

"That's a lot of land," said Pa. "I couldn't take care of that much land."

"We could try," said Trygve.

All afternoon the wagon rolled westward. They left the river, passed the fort, and kept going. They came out of the woods and found grass growing almost as high as the wagon.

"I wonder where we should settle," said Pa. "On the grassland or in the woods."

"Maybe both," said Rebekka. "We need to be near water and trees and...and...and there's a man over there and he's looking at us."

"He's an Indian," said Trygve. "He has dark skin and an Indian haircut."

"You all get inside the wagon," said Pa. "I'll handle this."

They crawled into the back of the wagon. "I hope they don't scalp us," said Rolf.

"I hear they do terrible things to women," said Signe as she crawled under the quilts. "Get under here," she said to Rebekka." Rebekka and baby Carrie hid under the quilts too.

Trygve listened.

"Hello," yelled the Indian.

"Hello," said Pa back to him.

"You looking for land?"

"Yes," said Pa.

"You go that way," said the Indian. "and you'll come to good land. There's water, and trees, and good land."

"Thank you," said Pa.

Rebekka and Signe threw the quilt off. "I feel silly," said Rebekka.

"I imagine there're good and bad Indians," said Signe.

Pa snapped the whip and called out "Gee!", and the oxen left the trail and slowly headed northward over a new growth of grass that was pushing its way through mounds of dead grass left over from  last year. They were headed toward a grove of trees. When they reached the trees, Pa got down and Trygve followed him. They walked into the woods and discovered a brook. They stood silently, watching the water run over the rocks.

"This is the place," said Pa. "We can start to unload the wagon."

"Our woods and our land," said Trygve, with reverence in his voice like it was a sacred thing.

"Yes," said Pa. "This will be ours." Pa stood with his hands on his hips, looking around. "We'll build our first house into the side of that hill. It will face south and be warm in the wintertime."

They started unloading the wagon. After the new purchases came the bedding, boxes and crates. Then Trygve helped Pa lift down the stove. They placed it on the ground. Rebekka said to Rolf and Signe, "Gather up some firewood, and I will bake some bread. Making supper will surely be easier with a stove."

Next Pa and Trygve lifted down the tool box, and on the very bottom was the new two-man saw that Pa had purchased before they left Iowa. "First thing we'll do is cut down a tree and build us a table for eating and working on. Then we'll build a lean-to to keep stuff dry."

They went into the woods and stopped by a dead white oak. Its trunk was about fourteen inches wide. "This will make a good table," said Pa. Trygve took one end of the saw, and together they went back and forth until the tree fell. Then they cut four six-foot lengths. Into the six-foot logs, he placed wedges, and with a mallet he split them in two. Together they carried the half logs back to the wagon. Then they went back to the downed tree, and with the hand saw Pa cut the legs for the table from some sturdy branches.

He said to Trygve, "While I work on this table, you go get us some supper." Trygve took the muzzle loader and some shot and walked toward the woods. Rolf followed behind him, gathering twigs for a fire.

Rolf walked back to the family carrying an armful of kindling, and Trygve decided to do a little exploring while he hunted for that night's supper. He began to follow a deer trail. He said to himself, "I shouldn't get lost if I stay on this trail. He saw some squirrel but said, "No. I'd rather have rabbit or prairie chicken."

He walked the trail for almost an hour before he saw a nice fat rabbit. He shot it and turned around to head back. He started running and then stopped. There were two trails going in two different directions. He hadn't noticed that there were two trails before, and he wondered which one he should take. He said, "I'll take the left one and if I don't come to the clearing, then I'll come back and take the right."

After about fifteen minutes he came to a tree across the path. "This wasn't here when I came," he said and he turned around and ran to where the paths came together and hurried back toward the homesite.

As he got close he could hear Signe calling, "Trygve, Trygve."

"I'm coming," he shouted back.

As he came out of the woods, Pa met him and said, "Where have you been?"

"I was looking for prairie chicken, and I got lost."

"You shouldn't have gone so far, and I needed your help with the table."

Rebekka interrupted, "Jon, don't be hard on him. Every day he catches meat for our supper."

"You're right," said Pa, and he turned around and walked back to the table.

Rebekka said, "We were worried about you."

"I was just a little bit lost."

"But we were worried," said Rebekka.

Rebekka sticking up for him made him feel good and reminded him of his Ma.

There was already smoke coming out of the stove, and Trygve skinned the rabbit and handed it to Rebekka. Then he walked over to Pa.

Pa had the four pieces notched together on a smaller log and had made four holes on the corners. He said to Trygve. "I want you to whittle the ends of the legs and make them fit into these holes." While Trygve whittled, Pa put together two benches, and while Trygve whittled the bench legs, Signe milked Viola.

By the time the sun was low in the sky, the table and benches were ready for their first meal on their Dakota homestead.

After supper, Trygve and Pa headed back to the tree and sawed off limbs to build the lean-to. They carried two eight-foot limbs and two six-foot limbs back to their homesite. They dug out holes and put the limbs upright, then connected them with smaller limbs. Before they could

**115**

finish, nightfall approached, and it started to turn dark and mosquitoes started buzzing.

"I want to sleep outside," said Trygve.

"Me too," said Signe, and they gathered piles of last year's dead grass and put their blankets on top and laid down as the stars started to come out.

Trygve was quiet. Signe asked, "Are you asleep?"

"No," answered Trygve.

"You're missing Ma. Aren't you."

"Yes," said Trygve.

"I am, too," she said.

"I wonder if Pa still thinks about her," said Trygve.

"I don't know," said Signe. "But there's mosquitoes here, and they're biting me."

As the night grew darker, the buzzing of the mosquitoes became louder and louder, and they pulled their blankets over their heads and soon fell asleep.

During the night, thunder sounded in the distance. Trygve woke up and felt large drops of rain on his forehead. "Come on, Signe," he said. "Let's get in the wagon."

Toward morning they woke up to feel a large animal pushing against the wagon. Pa sat up and said, "It's a bear. He smells the bread. Trygve, get the gun."

Rebekka said, "Everybody scream! We'll scare him away." They all screamed as loud as they could. Trygve lifted the flap and peeked out. Two black bears were running toward the woods.

"That's using your head," Pa said to Rebekka.

"We'll have to build a fire at night to keep the animals away," said Pa.

"Or we could try pulling the wagon away from the woods to the other side of our land," said Rebekka.

"Maybe," said Pa.

Trygve thought to himself, *She's smart. She thinks of everything.*

Trygve woke up to hear Pa yelling, "Come up," to the oxen. He already had them hooked up to the plow and was beginning to break the land. Trygve crawled to the end of the wagon and jumped down. Rebekka had already taken the dry kindling from under the wagon and was starting a fire in the stove. "Maybe we'll try to keep a fire going all night," she said. "It would be easier than making a new one every morning. "

"Good idea," said Trygve.

By the time the oatmeal was cooked and Viola was milked, Pa had plowed a garden spot. "It looks like real good soil," he said.

"As good as Iowa?" asked Trygve.

"I think so," said Pa.

After breakfast Pa went over the garden spot a second time while Rebekka and Signe cut up potatoes for seed. "Try to have one or two eyes in each piece," said Rebekka.

Trygve followed behind Pa with the hoe, breaking up the big clumps of dirt. Then, while Signe continued to cut potatoes, Rebekka followed behind Trygve and raked up the weeds and grass roots. "I'm getting a blister," said Trygve.

"You don't need to," said Rebekka. "I'll get socks to protect our hands." Signe brought a pail of cut-up potatoes over to Rebekka and Trygve. "Maybe we should trade off," said Rebekka, "so it won't be so tiresome. First we'll get

**118**

another pail of potatoes cut. Trygve, do you want to help cut potatoes?"

"Sure," said Trygve. He sat at the table cutting potatoes and watching Rolf follow Carrie in circles.

"Rebekka sure makes our work easier," said Signe.

"She does," admitted Trygve.

"Do you think she's getting fat?" asked Signe. "Like she's going to have a baby?"

"Maybe," answered Trygve. He was silent for a while and then he said, "I sure hope she doesn't die."

"Me, too," said Signe.

Before supper the whole garden was planted, and Pa had plowed and seeded a whole acre of wheat. After supper they all worked together to finish building the lean-to.

Then they all pushed the wagon, with Carrie in it, to a spot away from the woods. "If the bears come tonight, we'll just scream," said Pa.

○　○　○

After four weeks and four days had gone by, there were twelve acres of wheat beginning to sprout and ten acres of oats planted, along with an acre of corn and five acres of barley. The potatoes, peas, beans, carrots, lettuce, spinach, and rutabogas were all several inches high.

"Starting next week we should be able to start eating the spinach and lettuce," said Rebekka.

Pa stood with his hands on his hips, looking at his fields full of young, tender plants. "The season is getting too late to plant any more."

"It's far more than what we had in Norway," said Trygve. "We will have lots to eat all winter."

"Yes," said Pa. "And if we have good weather, we should have plenty for next winter and seed for next spring, and some left over to sell. Now we can build ourselves a house."

"Starting today?" asked Trygve.

"First there are some things I need to get from town, and I will need the wagon," said Pa. "We're going to take the top off and set it on the ground so you all will have a dry place in case it rains."

Trygve helped Pa carry the boards from the wagon and place them on the ground. Then he spread the feather ticks and blankets over them. Rebekka and Signe helped Pa and Trygve move the topper onto the boards and blankets.

"Can I go with you?" asked Trygve.

"No," said Pa. "I need you to stay and protect them. You're the only one who is good with the gun."

"Why can't all of us go?" asked Trygve.

"Someone needs to be here to protect our claim," said Pa. "Anyway, there is something I need to do all alone."

"How long will you be gone?" asked Trygve.

"I should be home tomorrow evening," said Pa, "or the next day. Depends on how long it takes for me to get the things we need."

Trygve watched Pa disappear into the swaying grass. He turned around and looked at Rebekka and Signe kneading bread in the large wooden bowl that rested on a tree stump. Rolf and Carrie were lying on top of blankets on the table. Carrie was almost asleep.

"I need some water," said Rebekka.

"I'll get some," said Signe.

"Me too," said Rolf, and he picked up the pail and he and Signe started walking toward the woods where the stream flowed.

Being alone with Rebekka made Trygve feel uncomfortable. So far he had managed to avoid her. But Carrie was asleep, and it was just the two of them. What if she tried to talk to him?

"A person could get kind of lonely out here with nobody but family to talk to," said Rebekka.

"Yes," said Trygve. "It would be nice to have some neighbors."

"I wonder how long before others will come," said Rebekka. "I miss not having any women folk to talk to. And I miss church."

"I don't miss church at all," said Trygve. "I hate God."

"What?" asked Rebekka.

"Yes, I said I hate God," said Trygve. "The captain said that I mustn't cry because it was God's will that Ma died. So I hate God for making her die."

"Trygve," said Rebekka. "The captain must not have the same God that I have. The God that I believe in never

**121**

wills death. He desires that each one of us be healthy and happy."

"Then why did she die?" asked Trygve.

"Because ever since Adam and Eve ate the apple, this world has been a mixed-up place," answered Rebekka. "I think God cried with us when your Ma died."

"Did you cry?" asked Trygve.

"Yes," said Rebekka. "She was the dearest friend I ever had. I cried when she left Norway, and I cried again when I got your father's letter."

"Then why did you come over and marry Pa?"

"It was something I had to do for Gro," said Rebekka. "It's the last thing I could do for her....take care of her family. I have come to love your Pa and you children but I came because of my love for her."

"Oh," said Trygve.

"Trygve," said Rebekka. "Do you know what I think you need to do?"

"What?" said Trygve.

"Go off by yourself and remember your Ma," said Rebekka. "Remember everything you can about her and even talk to her."

Trygve stood looking at the ground. Rebekka came over to him and put her arm on his shoulder and said, "And remember it's okay for a young man to cry."

Trygve shrugged her arm from his shoulder and picked up his fishing pole and headed for the creek. He wasn't thinking about fishing, but he wanted it to look like he was.

He came to an open place by the stream and lay down in the grass and looked up at the sky. He watched the clouds go by and thought about his Ma. Rebekka had said to remember everything about her. He remembered how she used to cuddle him in her lap when he was little and sing to him. He remembered how she looked, and how she stuck up for him when he was in trouble.

The memories flooded over him and he turned over in the grass and said, "Ma, why did you have to leave us." He laid there with his head in his arms and sobbed. "I miss you, Ma," he whispered, and he fell asleep.

When he woke up there were long shadows in the woods. He stood up slowly and said to himself, "I really should catch some fish for supper." Very soon he had four fish and started slowly walking back.

Trygve wondered who he should believe. Was God like the captain said or like Rebekka said? The captain's answer to his pain had been too easy. It was cheap talk because he had come to it without any effort.

At least Rebekka had entered into his pain. She had cried too, and had listened to him and cared about all of them. "Well, God," he said out loud, "who should I believe?" Then he shouted, "GOD, WHY DON'T YOU SHOW ME A SIGN?"

It was as if an answer formed inside of him. It whispered, "I sent you Rebekka."

When he got back to their place he saw another wagon and two Indian women. "I should have been here to protect them," he said to himself. As he drew near, the Indian women left. Signe looked scared, and Rolf was hiding behind the wood pile.

"Are you alright?" he asked Rebekka.

"We're fine," she said. "They just wanted a few chickens and some bread."

"Did you give it to them?" asked Trygve.

"Yes," said Rebekka. "At the McCawleyville store they told us that when the Indians came and asked for something, we should give it to them because when they left it would be gone anyway."

"So we're supposed to give them everything they ask for?" said Trygve.

"They didn't want very much," said Rebekka. "And it helps for us to remember that all of this land belonged to them before the white man came."

"And I guess it helps for us to be friendly with them," said Trygve. "But I hope they don't come back for the rest of the chickens."

Late the next afternoon Trygve saw Pa coming with the wagon. Signe and Rolf came running and they waited for him to come into the yard. They wanted to see what was in the wagon.

As the oxen stopped, Pa jumped into the back of the wagon and picked up a tan puppy. Rolf squealed with delight. Pa said, "I figured we could use a dog to scare off the bears and coons."

"And he'll be a good companion for Rolf," said Rebekka.

"I see you bought two windows and a door," said Trygve, looking into the wagon. "And nails and another barrel of flour and...uh...what is that?" He pointed at a white marble slab lying on the bottom of the wagon.

"It's a memorial for your Ma," said Pa. "When I realized she was dying, I cut off a lock of her hair for us to remember her by. We are going to bury it here. This is the place she dreamed of."

He reached inside his vest and pulled out a small brown bag and opened it for them all to see. Rebekka touched the blonde curl and said, "It's just like I remembered it." A tear rolled down her cheek. "Gro always had the prettiest hair of anyone."

Pa handed the little bag to Signe, who held it like it was a sacred thing. Then he picked up the slab and said to Trygve, "Get the shovel. We will bury it now."

Trygve walked over and picked up the shovel and followed Pa and the others to the edge of the woods. When they got there Pa took the shovel from Trygve and dug a hole about a foot deep and three feet wide. Then he took the little brown bag from Signe and placed it at the bottom of the hole. On top he placed the white marble gravestone.

They all stood back and looked at it while Pa read out the inscription:

Gro Ytterhorn
June 14, 1836-May 18, 1867
Buried here is a lock of hair
from our beloved

who died from childbirth and
now rests on the ocean floor.
May her memory bless us always.

When he was through putting the dirt around the memorial he said, "Rebekka, could you sing us a song?"

Rebekka wiped her tears away and began to sing, "Behold a host arrayed in white..." Then they said the Lord's Prayer.

"We will think of this as your Ma's grave," said Pa. "Go and find some flowers for it."

Trygve and Signe walked through the grass on a deer trail gathering bluebells, daisies, and other flowers. When their arms were so full that they couldn't hold any more they turned back. When they came to the grave, they dropped the flowers in front of the memorial.

"Let's bring flowers every year on her birthday," said Signe.

"Yes," said Trygve. "Her memory will live with us forever."

As they walked back to the table they could smell coffee brewing. The rough table was covered with Rebekka's best linen tablecloth. On the table were the blue and white sugar bowl and creamer and the four cups and saucers.

Rebekka said, "Shall we have some coffee?"